Snow Blacc
& the seven Thugs

BY: RUBY

D1524354

Snow Blacc   **Ruby**

Chapter One
EIGHT YEARS EARLIER

My name is Snow Blacc, and I know y'all are trying to figure out how my name came about so I'll fill y'all in before I tell my story. I was born the first day of winter. My mother said the night her water broke the news forecast said we were going to have a blizzard and that night it was the worst snowstorm Michigan had seen in almost a decade. My mother wanted to name me Winter, but my father decided on Snow. I got made fun of as a child about my name, but it didn't bother me, I thought it was unique.

I know y'all probably thinking about Snow White and the dwarfs when you hear my name, but this here story is about me and my seven older brothers that were once good boys but turned into thugs the morning my parents died. After our parents' deaths, we had to make a way so my brothers fell to the streets, especially my oldest brother Aaron. They built a crew called Blacc Boys INC. My father was soft and he liked to gamble, but my brothers showed the streets they were nothing like my father. However, my brother Aaron used most of his money to put me through school and take care of my younger brothers until they were eighteen, and sometimes I took that for granted...

$$$$$

"Snow, bring your little ass here right now," I heard my mother yell from the living room.

I walked into the living room already knowing why she wanted me but I played it cool.

"Yes, Mom," I answered in a bold tone waiting on her to respond.

"What did I tell you about stealing candy canes from the tree?" she said, glaring at me with a smile on her beautiful, brown, round face.

"To take from the back of the tree, but I swear I haven't been taking them," I answered truthfully.

I stood there admiring my beautiful mother. For her to have seven boys and one girl she didn't look stressed or sleepy, not one bit. My daddy kept her laced in the nicest gear a girl could have. She was spoiled and she deserved everything my dad did for her.

"Ma, could we please make one stop today? I know it's crazy out there, but I still have to get Daddy a gift. Where is he at anyway?" I asked as I looked around, noticing the boys were gone too.

"Yes, I'll take you. Go get dressed and I'll meet you in the garage in seven minutes tops, Snow. I'm not waiting on you all day. I still have to get back and start Christmas dinner and prepare to make cookies," she explained as she walked off.

I went to my bedroom and put on a red PINK jogger with my brand-new wheat UGG boots my daddy bought me for my birthday last week. I pulled my headscarf off to let my feed in braids breathe. Once I was done, I headed downstairs and stopped in my tracks when I heard my mother screaming at the top of her lungs. She told me to never eavesdrop on her conversations, but it was something about the conversation she was having. It was intense, and I rarely heard my mother raise her voice.

"What the fuck do you mean you owe him fifty grand? We don't have that type of money laying around. You said you were done gambling Aaron!" my mother shouted into the phone before hanging up.

I heard everything standing in the foyer, but I had to act like I didn't hear anything. The last thing I needed was her jumping down my throat. I finally made it downstairs.

"Are you okay, Mom? I heard yelling," I asked her with a worried look on my face.

"I'm okay, Snow, don't worry your pretty little face, baby girl. Your daddy can really get underneath my skin at times, that's all," she confessed while staring at me.

I had the perfect little life. We lived in Forest Hills right outside of Grand Rapids, Michigan. I loved going to the mall but it was so far away. The drive was long to me, thirty minutes to be exact. We made it to the Rolex store and it was packed. I asked my mother if she wanted to go in with me but she declined. After spending an hour in the store, I found my daddy the perfect watch. I got it engraved with a short message. "Daddy's little girl, love Snow B." I walked out of the jewelry store happy until I noticed my mom crying. I got in the car with concerned eyes.

"Mom, why are you crying?" I uttered.

"I'm a little stressed out, that's all. Don't worry about me. Did you find your daddy a nice gift?" she mumbled.

"Yes," I replied.

"Good, now let's get home so we can get this dinner started. It's Christmas Eve; we should be listening to music and drinking eggnog," she blurted out.

I laughed because I knew she was serious. That's why I loved my mom; she knew how to turn a bad situation into a good one. When we made it home my dad's truck was parked out in the driveway. I got irritated because I knew my brothers were in there running ragged. We walked into the house and ran into a strange looking man who was with my daddy. I whispered to my mom, "Who is that man?" Snow asked.

"I don't know. Maybe one of your dad's friends from back in the day," she whispered.

"Luke, this is my wife and my only daughter Snow," my daddy spoke.

"Nice to meet you gorgeous ladies," he softly spoke as he shook our hands. It was something about him; his energy was off and I didn't like it.

My mother and I went to the kitchen prepping to start our Christmas dinner for tomorrow night. In the midst of prepping, my daddy ordered Chinese food. We ate and listened to their crazy stories about them growing up and how their Christmas used to be. Once we finished dinner my mom and I made cookies and listened to Christmas music while dancing around the kitchen. Once the cookies were done, we sat down in the living room around the tree talking, opening one gift each. I opened my gift and my mouth dropped. It was a Tiffany bracelet and matching earrings.

"Oh my god, thank you, Mom and Dad." I jumped up off the couch kissing both of them on the cheeks.

I was officially popping now. I noticed it had a charm on it that read *"Blacc forever EST 12/21/96."* My daddy and mom always went all out for me.

I went up to my room, took a nice, hot shower and wrapped my hair before laying down in bed. I heard a knock at the door and I just knew it was my mother and father coming to say goodnight.

"Goodnight, baby girl, we love you and see you in the morning." My dad kissed me on the forehead.

I laid there thinking about how Christmas Day was going to go until I drifted off into a deep slumber.

Christmas Day...

"Wake up! Wake up!" I screamed in the hallway banging on everybody's door waking them. I noticed my parents weren't up yet which was strange. I stood in front of their door banging hard and loud.

"It's Christmas, wake up!" I yelled through the door.

No one came to the door. I walked into my parents' room. Before I made it to the bed, the smell of fresh blood hit my nose.

"Mommy?" I said, almost stuttering.

When I made it to the bed, I found my mother's lifeless body lying in a pool of blood with her eyes open. I screamed and dropped to my knees trying to wake her up.

"Wake up, Mommy, please wake up!" I uttered with tears flooding my face.

I heard screaming coming from downstairs and I took off running. When I made it downstairs, I found my daddy with his brains on our white Christmas tree and fireplace. My oldest brother Aaron was standing over his body with a look of shock. I never in my life felt so sick to my stomach. My knees got weak and I buckled. I got lightheaded and everything went black; I passed out. Last thing I remember was my brothers trying to catch me. The paramedics had finally arrived waking me up but unfortunately, my parents never woke up. My life was never same after that night. After years of trying to get it together and forget about the past, it didn't work. When seeing your parents dead on Christmas Day, you have no choice but to say fuck the holidays. All it brought back was cold memories of my father's brains splattered.

Chapter Two
WINTER 2017

I walked into my law office and I noticed Christmas decorations were up and we were still in the month of November. I had a feeling my secretary had something to do with this and it pissed me off. I instantly got upset.

"Lysa, who decorated my office without my permission?" I yelled at her, causing her to turn red in the face.

"I'm sorry, Ms. Blacc, I thought it was okay to do. It's the holiday season, so I was trying to brighten up the place. We need to get in the holiday spirit around here. You've been in a funk lately," she answered honestly.

"Take it down, or you're fired." I walked past her into my office, slamming the door. I hated Christmas. The holidays brought up old memories I didn't want to think about.

Lysa came across my intercom.

"Line one, Snow," Lysa uttered.

I wasn't in the mood to talk to anyone. I had three cases today at 61st district court, and all my cases had me stressed out. I buzzed Lysa back.

"Could you please take a message? I'm getting ready to head out for court soon and I don't need the extra stress," I spat.

"It's your brother Aaron. Please take the call, it sounded very important. No one deserves to spend the holidays by themselves, Ms. Blacc." She hung the phone up leaving me to think about what she said.

I got up from my desk, grabbing my MK briefcase and coat, and headed for the door. I was exhausted from being up all night reviewing my cases.

When I made it downstairs my driver was already waiting on me. I just knew traffic was going to be horrible and backed up. People were born and raised in Michigan and still didn't know how to drive. We sat in traffic for almost twenty minutes before making it to the courthouse.

I was in a rush trying to get in the courthouse when a man bumped me, knocking all of my paperwork out of my hands. The pavement was wet from the snow and my paperwork was soaked.

"Watch where the fuck you're going!" I screamed at the man hovering over me.

"My bad young lady, I didn't see you. I'm late for work and I didn't mean for this to happen to you," he explained.

"I don't care, watch what you're doing next time," I ranted, picking my paperwork up heading into the building.

"Yeah, whatever," he stated and walked away.

Court was dragging. Two of my cases went to trial. My third case pled guilty. Once court ended I ran out of there. I needed a hot bubble bath with some strawberry moscato wine. I had to make my driver stop at Pierre's Market on my way home.

"Could you please stop at Pierre's Market on the way to my house?" I asked, rolling the back window down.

"Yes, Ms. Blacc," my driver responded.

My driver pulled up to Pierre's Market and I sat there looking at the families picking out Christmas trees. I took a deep breath before getting out the car. I walked into the market, running into the same man from the courthouse.

"So, you're stalking me now?" I asked, staring him down.

"What makes you think that, sweetheart? Because I'm at the same grocery store minding my own business. I see nothing wrong with going to the store. You are one rude bitch and I'm trying my hardest not to cuss you out," he mumbled.

"A bitch huh? You don't know me or know what the fuck kind of day I've been through so don't use that word too loosely, my nigga," I barked at him walking off towards the wines and deli section. I was over today and his rude ass. Trying to pick out wine, I felt bad talking to that man like that. I heard my mother in my head.

Go apologize to that man now, I heard her say clear as day. But I kept walking, not listening to my mother in my head. I missed her so much, and I knew missing her was making me bitter. But it was so hard for me even after eight years. In the summer I was a happy camper. But soon as fall season rolled around, the depression kicked in.

I paid for my things and headed for the door when I felt a hand land on my arm. I was getting ready to go off until I saw it was the mysterious man again and this time, he was actually being nice.

"Look, I just wanted to apologize for calling you out of your name. I'm sorry, you didn't deserve that. I'm a man, I can admit when I'm wrong. I know this might seem strange, but since we keep bumping into each other, my name is Pierre," he said looking in my eyes.

"I'm Snow and I'm sorry for being rude also. I've been stressed out dealing with work and you didn't deserve that type of attitude from me. Please forgive me," I pleaded.

I didn't notice it earlier but the man standing before me was fine as hell. He was tall and dark-skinned with nice, pink lips. I had to stop looking at him. He walked me out to my car putting my groceries in the trunk.

"Thank you," I mumbled.

"You're welcome, Ms. Snow. I hope to see you again, hopefully under better circumstances," he chuckled walking back into the store. The whole ride home I thought about Pierre. He was sexy but I knew we could never be. I quickly pushed the thought to the back of my mind.

Chapter Three

THE SEVEN THUGS: AARON

"I tried calling Snow's office and her cellphone, but she hasn't returned a call. We need to go check on her; you know she gets a little crazy during Christmas time," I gritted at my brothers. I looked around the room looking at Marcus, Devon, Nico, Drew, Peter and Paul as they all sat there with a blank looks on their faces.

After our parents died, I chose to raise my seven younger siblings. Since I was the oldest and my father's Jr, I didn't want them growing up in the system so I took them under my wing. I knew my dad would turn in his grave if he knew they were in foster care.

I got up from my desk looking at my six brothers, thanking God for watching over us after all these years. We'd been through some shit but we had each other's backs. We were the biggest drug suppliers in Michigan, "Blacc Boys Inc." I ran shit the way I saw fit. I raised Snow to the best of my ability but I felt it wasn't enough. She didn't have to worry about paying for anything. I put my life on hold so they could live comfortably and now I couldn't get a phone call in return.

"I need for the twins to put eyes on Snow while Devon and Marcus run the meeting with the boys," I barked orders looking at them. No one spoke, they just nodded their heads letting me know they were listening. Paul looked at Peter then looked at me and spoke.

"Aaron, if Snow don't want to be bothered then let her stuck up ass be. She'll soon realize you tried to do good by her!" Paul yelled out catching everyone off guard because he never really talked since our parents died.

"She has no choice but to talk to me. We are family and I miss my baby sister just like I know y'all niggas do. Her birthday will be coming up soon and I need all of y'all to pitch in and help so we can pull this off together. It's time to bring Snow home," my voice boomed through the office.

"My wife Desari and I are planning her a birthday at the Flats Hotel so please don't fuck it up by running y'all mouth around town."

My baby brother Paul got up from his seat, walking out of the conference room. I decided to go after him.

"What's wrong, Paul? You got that look and I don't like it," I confessed, glaring at him.

"I got a lead on who killed Mom and Dad," he spat.

"You what?"

"You heard me, Aaron. I know who killed Mom and Dad. It was that bitch ass nigga Luke he owed fifty grand to before Christmas. Dad had the money but he killed him and Mom anyway. Niggas are talking on the streets, bro, because this nigga Luke is getting reckless. I'm going after this nigga and his whole family once my people get back to me," he ranted.

I couldn't lie; that shit fucked my head up. I stood there staring at Paul. I saw stress in his eyes and I could tell he meant business. I broke the silence, speaking.

"You don't need to wait for nobody when you got your bros; this is personal. We all are hurting and have been trying to find the pussy niggas who did this to our parents. Please don't do anything stupid with anybody you don't know," I mumbled.

"Yeah, we'll see," he mumbled walking off. I figured I'd call him later and check on him. That news he had just told me was big and something he had to probably let sink in alone.

I walked back into the conference room with the rest of my brothers. I was ready to go home after receiving that bomb Paul dropped on me, but I knew I had to tell them. And one by one, after I told them the news, they went from my quiet little brothers to goons. I had been keeping my brothers quiet and in control for years, but now I knew they were about to come out their shells.

"Whatever you need us to do, we are there, bro. I been waiting to hear this news for a long time," my brother Peter spoke up and said. The rest of my brothers nodded as well.

"I'll let y'all know everything as the days go by. It's the holidays and I don't want none of us getting killed, and make sure Snow isn't caught in the crossfire. I know she has been distant but I promise she will come around. Y'all know that shit with our parents ruined Christmas season for her. So in the meantime, lay low but keep your eyes open. I'm about to head to the house." I stood up from my chair. I wanted to go home and lay with my wifey. She was too crazy and she was the only one that could soothe me.

"Well, we all leaving out at the same time, my nigga. You not about to leave us here looking like we broke in," Peter yelled across the room making a nigga smile. I loved how my brothers had my back.

Paul and Peter were one year older than Snow, but you couldn't tell they were twins since they were so opposite of each other. One was light-skinned like our mom and the other dark-skinned like our father. We called them "Twin"; it was better than calling them by their names.

"Alright bet. I'll meet y'all in the lobby." I grabbed my jacket from my office chair and headed to the elevator.

"Where Paul go, Aaron?" Peter asked while looking around the elevator.

"He said he had some shit to handle, he'll holler at us later," I lied through my teeth. I knew my brother was pissed off and probably on his own mission. I knew if I told his twin the truth, he would go into beast mode too. I needed my hot head brothers to follow my lead so I couldn't tell them what each other was doing.

I made it to the lobby in record time, the elevator doors were just opening. When we got off the elevator, I noticed a black XL Yukon with tinted windows just sitting there. Something didn't feel right. I pulled my strap from behind my back and signaled my brother to do the same.

"Get down!" I yelled as I dropped to the floor.

Shots started ringing, shattering the glass windows of the office building I rented. For the first time in my life, I had been caught slipping. We returned fire hitting at least two of the gunmen. The truck took off and left two of their men behind. I got off the floor and walked over to the man who was still alive yelling bloody murder.

"Who the fuck sent you, my nigga?" I yelled with my gun pointed at his head.

"Nigga, fuck you, I'm going to die anyways so why should I tell you, pussy nigga!" he shouted, spiting blood into my face. I let off three shots to his dome.

I looked at my youngest brother, Marcus, telling him what to do.

"Call Paul and tell him to meet us at my house. Get the cleaning crew down here now and delete the footage from the camera system. Find out who sent these bitch ass niggas too! I bet it was that bitch ass nigga Pierre!" I hollered at my brothers. I then walked out to the parking lot and jumped in my truck. I pulled out the parking lot with fire in my eyes from anger. I was mad as hell and I was bloody. As I drove home, I realized I had been shot.

"Fuck!" I said to myself as I grabbed my arm. I knew my wife was going to be angry and scared, but I knew I had to head home for her help. There was no way I was going to the hospital and getting the opps involved.

Later that evening
SNOW

I sat in my jet bath relaxing, listening to Pandora, when my phone started ringing off the hook. I tried to ignore it but whoever it was kept calling so I got out of the tub irritated, answering the phone.

"Twin, why are you blowing my fucking phone up like that? If I didn't answer the first few times that was telling you something, damn." I sucked my teeth. It was my brother Paul and I wasn't in the mood to talk.

"I didn't call to argue, Snow. You need to get to Aaron's house ASAP. We just got shot at leaving Tower Heights," he snapped, and then hung up in my face. It felt like déjà vu all over again from the day I found my parents. I got out the tub and dressed. I started thinking the worst. I prayed my brother was okay. I rarely spoke to them but I would hate if something happened to them.

I hated driving in the icy roads but I had no choice. I jumped into my Jeep Wrangler and hit 75 mph on Highway 131 trying to make it to Aaron's house. I prayed to God no one was hurt. I pulled into Aaron's driveway and saw all my brothers' cars. I parked my truck and jumped out. I ran to the door, almost beating it down until his wife Desari opened the door with tears in her eyes.

"Omg, Snow, it's so nice to see you after so long," she pulled me into a hug and cried.

"What's going on, Dezzy? Where are my brothers? Are they okay?" I had so many questions. I walked into the house finding them in the kitchen.

"What the fuck, Aaron?" I shouted while my voice cracked from being emotional.

Aaron looked at me with bloodshot red eyes while holding his shoulder. He didn't look like himself. I saw my other siblings sitting around with the look of murder on their faces. Aaron finally spoke, breaking the silence.

"We got shot at tonight and I was hit in the shoulder. Before that though, Paul came to me with some important information pertaining to our parents' death. He told me he knows who did it and I told him not to pursue the mission until we had all of our facts. Somebody has to know that we know who killed our parents and they didn't want us to find out. They tried to kill us tonight because I found out," Aaron was telling me a mouthful. I was shocked they had finally cracked the case.

"What, then why is the muthafucka who killed our parents still breathing, and who is he? I want his ass dead. Their family needs to feel the same pain we've endured over the last eight years. I don't care how you kill them. Burn the city down if you have to," I cried my eyes out. All seven of my brothers hugged me.

"Don't cry, Snow. We gonna handle this shit. You don't need to worry about who it was, just know Mom and Pops is going to be able to rest in peace soon," Aaron assured me.

We sat there talking, catching up on life. I didn't realize how much I missed my brothers until now. Aaron look and acted just like our father, Aaron Sr. I felt the love I once felt years ago. I noticed my brother Paul was staring at me and it made me uncomfortable.

"Why you staring at me like that, twin?" I asked, staring daggers into him.

"I just want to know why you abandoned us like we weren't family, Snow?" he asked, getting emotional.

"I never abandoned y'all. Momma and Daddy's death took a toll on me and I needed to get myself together. I had to push myself," I blurted out.

"That's some bullshit, Snow, and you know it. We all lost Mom and Dad, not just you. You just a stuck up ass bitch, acting like you better than us and you're not," he barked, getting up from his seat walking out of the kitchen.

I sat there thinking about what my brother said and I felt bad. I probably was being a selfish bitch. I didn't consider their feelings. I had to swallow my pride and talk to twin. I didn't want him to ever feel like I didn't care or that I was too good, because I wasn't. I looked at my brothers and let them know I'd be back. I had to talk to twin.

"Hey, I'll be back. I need to talk to him alone," I mumbled, walking off to find twin.

I walked around Aaron's house until I found twin in the family room. You would think we'd be close since we were a year apart.

"Twin, can we please talk?" I whispered, walking into the family room.

"Yeah, say what you gotta say," he said nonchalantly.

"Look, Paul, I'm sorry that you feel that way. I never wanted to make you feel like I didn't care and I'm sorry for that. You and Peter are closer to me than the other boys. I would give my life for y'all," my voice cracked, getting emotional. I sat there looking at my brother. He was broken and I didn't like that he thought I abandoned him. We sat there catching up on our personal lives. I felt so bad I strayed away from my brothers. Paul rolled a blunt telling everything and I enjoyed every moment of it.

When I looked at my watch, I noticed it was almost one in the morning. I gave Paul a hug and headed for the door.

"I have to get out of here, but I promise I'll be in touch, and tell the boys I went home for the night. I love y'all, be safe."

I left out of the house and decided to go for a drink at Perfection Lounge. I needed to be in somebody's bar getting drunk. My life was starting to feel like I was in the Matrix. I drove downtown parking my Jeep right outside. I walked into the bar and it was a slow one, which was a bounce for me. I could get drunk without bitches stepping on my feet. When I walked in I noticed my favorite bartender was in there working.

"What's up, girl, what you drinking?" my favorite bartender said to me. Her name was Maria. She was a short Hispanic girl with long, blonde hair. She talked with a bit of an accent but I understood her clearly.

"Let me get a margarita and two shots of Patron on the side."

Maria raised her eyebrow and smirked. "Somebody trying to get fucked up."

"Girl, my life is cray right now. This probably isn't going to be enough." I sighed.

"Alright, girl. Well I'ma throw in two more shots on the house, since it's the holiday season." She smiled.

"Yeah, thanks," I responded in a bitter tone.

I sat there drinking my drink, thinking about everything that was going on in my life. My parents' killers were found; that was a big shock to me. Ever since that day, we hadn't heard anything. The case was closed and nobody had a clue. Now shit was about to get real. Whoever it was, was going to die with no mercy.

Snow Blacc   **Ruby**

Chapter Four
I RUN THIS SHIT: PIERRE

I stood there yelling at my soldiers, not giving a damn how they felt. Niggas couldn't follow simple ass directions and it was starting to piss me the fuck off.

"I told y'all niggas not to fucking shoot. You niggas had one job and that was to snatch Aaron's bitch ass up and bring him to me alive!" I criticized them. "Where the fuck is Luke?" I yelled at one of my niggas. One of my little hitters finally spoke up breaking the silence.

"Yo, boss man, that nigga Luke is not to be trusted. He started shooting soon as ole boy got off the elevator. I tried to stop him but that nigga is reckless and you need me to handle him, uncle or not," he mumbled.

I looked around the room, looking at every last one of them niggas. I could see they were fed up with Luke's shit and so was I. I didn't know what was up with this nigga but I told him my beef with Aaron was mine and I wanted things to go my way. Aaron thought he was running shit, but I was ready to show him who was the real boss, but this nigga Luke was making sloppy moves on my time.

Everybody was dressed in all black. It was so quiet in the warehouse you could hear a pin drop. But I made my voice boom through the entire warehouse. I handpicked every nigga in my crew, but not Luke. He was my uncle, so he came with the shit since my business was a family business. He did ten years in prison because of him being reckless, not caring about shit. After my pops died, he started getting sloppy and when you get sloppy, you leave traces, and his ass got caught slacking back in the day. I didn't need that type of heat on me, not right now, or ever. This was my empire and I ran shit my way. I was smarter than him and my pops. I had to handle him soon and get him off my team.

"Well, when y'all see that nigga, tell him come holler at me. I'm about to get up out of here for the night. Make sure y'all keep your ears to the streets about that nigga Aaron. I bet he knows that was me," I uttered, pulling my pants up, walking off towards the door.

I was done for the night. That nigga Luke had fucked up my whole night and I wasn't feeling it. I needed a drink, fast. I pulled up to Perfection Lounge so I could drink and relax. I sat in the back where it was dark. I didn't want to be bothered with so I opened a tab so I could drink with no problem.

I sat there thinking about everything that's been happening in my life until I heard a female voice causing me to snap out of my thoughts.

"This can't be coincidental that we keep meeting like this," she yelped, putting her keys in her purse.

I looked at her sexy, chocolate ass talk. She was wearing a jogger suit that hugged all her curves. A nigga was slightly turned on for a minute. I had to tell my boy to calm down. I licked my lips staring at her. Shawty was bad. My words got caught in my throat for a minute before I found them clearing my throat.

"Nah, I think you're stalking me, Ma." I chuckled at my own joke. It was a corny ass reply but I wasn't expecting to run into shawty again. "Since you here you might as well sit down and have a drink with a nigga. You look stressed out," I invited her to sit with me. I can't lie; she was pretty as hell so I didn't know why her attitude was so nasty the first few times we bumped into each other.

"I am stressed out, but it's all good," she huffed and slid into the seat next to me.

"So are you single?" I asked her.

"Yes I am." She looked down at her drink.

"So, why are you single, Snow?" I hesitated for a couple minutes before asking her. She looked me in my eyes, taking a deep breath before talking.

"I just never really been pressed about dating. Relationships bring headaches and heartaches. Plus, I never really cared for a boyfriend. I've always been focused on my schooling and career. My daddy always talked to me about the three B's growing up, "Books before boys." That stuck with me throughout my entire life; plus I'm a virgin," she explained, taking another sip of her drink from her glass of wine.

"Are you single, Mr. Pierre?" she asked, twirling her finger on the rim of her wine glass, glaring at me.

"Yes I am," I smirked. But I felt a little lightheaded.

"Why are you single? You must be a cheater," she laughed.

I started thinking about my situation and I started feeling sick. Before I could answer her question, I started feeling queasy as fuck.

"I'm sorry, Snow, but I need to take a rain check. I have to go, I don't feel so good." I got up from the table and stumbled, almost falling to my knees. I saw Snow get up from her chair. All of a sudden, the room started to spin. I was fucked up, scrambling, looking for my keys. She must have gotten tired of seeing me struggle so she started helping me.

"I can't let you drive like this, Pierre," she softly spoke.

Taking my keys from my hand, Snow guided me across the street to the JW Marriot. She got a room on the seventh floor. I staggered onto the elevator and to the room. Reaching the door, I started throwing up. Snow flipped out.

"OMG!" she scoffed, opening the door. I had thrown up on her. She laid me down on the bed. She ran to the bathroom to clean herself up while I laid on the bed embarrassed and in agony.

I took my clothes off and walked to the bathroom not really knowing what was going on with me. I knew I needed some hot water on my body to sober me up. When I got in the bathroom, Snow was in the shower. I had thrown up like I was in the exorcist. It landed in her hair, on her clothes and probably her face. I felt bad I had done that, but I couldn't hold it in any longer. I stepped in the shower with her, and she quickly got out. She dried off and wrapped the white fluffy towel around her nice, curvy frame. I watched her blow dry her hair. She must have noticed I was staring at her because she started talking to me through the glass shower.

"Damn, boy you almost gave me a heart attack. Are you okay now?" She turned off the hair dryer.

"My bad, Ma. I didn't mean to scare you and I'm sorry for throwing up on you," I admitted. "I'm going through some real-life shit right now and I been bottling up all these emotions. Feel like my life swirling out of control, so I drank too much." I dropped my head ashamed, letting the water run on my body so I could sober up.

Snow opened the shower door and handed me a towel to dry off with. She stepped back, letting me get out the shower. She looked at me before breaking the silence between us.

"I guess I was so blinded by my own shit that I didn't realize anyone around me was going through shit. I should have asked how you were," she blurted out. She ran a washcloth under cold water and handed it to me.

"Here, this should wake you up." She noticed I was nodding off but I heard everything she had said.

I took the towel and went back into the room and Snow followed behind me. She needed to know why I was stressed out like this. I didn't look stressed at all; I hid that shit well. I sat down on the bed and patted it, asking her to sit next to me. She sat down and I opened up like a book. I was surprised, but it was something about Snow that I liked.

"You asked me why I was single earlier, so I need to tell you the real reason why." I dropped my head into my hands. "I've been battling the courts so I can get custody of my son. My baby mama living wild as fuck out here and she has him in the middle of it. She's money hungry so my child support went up. Not the fact that I even care, it's the principle she's not taking care of him. It hurts me because he's a child. He doesn't deserve this type of lifestyle; he's only five. I'm trying not to give up on my baby boy but I feel like I'm losing it." I broke down crying. I felt Snow put her hand over my shoulder letting me know she was there for me and that she saw me as a man and not a bitch. She spoke softly to me.

"I can't make any promises, Pierre, but I'm a lawyer. I might can help you if you allow me to. It's not a lot of fathers out here trying to raise their kids like you. You deserve to be in your son's life. I want to help you," she mumbled.

I kissed Snow, and I never kissed bitches in the mouth. That took me by surprise when I kissed her. I felt something that I never felt before. She sat there frozen. She didn't resist so I laid her on the bed. Her towel came open, and all I could do was stare at her sexy ass. I looked up at her and she looked nervous.

"You good, Snow?" I asked, looking her in her eyes.

"I'm okay, just nervous, that's all." She shivered like she was cold.

I went down, opening her legs. It was wild because I was getting ready to eat pussy on the first night. I kissed on her sweet nectar causing her to jump and her breathing picked up. She was trying her hardest to get away from me. I pulled her even closer, locking my arms around her thighs. She came back to back. I went to my jeans pocket pulling a condom out. Shawty looked scared when I put the condom on.

She had a nervous grin on her face before she asked me, "Where the fuck do you think you're putting that at?" She jumped up, gripping her towel.

"I'm not going to hurt you, Snow. Lay down and relax, Ma. I won't lie; it will hurt for a couple minutes," I convinced her to lay back down. "If it gets too painful just tell me to stop."

I tried easing my way into her sweet, warm, wet nectar. She moaned out in pain and pleasure. After that first round, I had her open. She begged me for more and I was happy because she had some drop. We fucked all night until we passed out. I woke up the next morning noticing Snow was gone. It was dry blood in the sheets and I then remembered shawty telling me she was a virgin. I got up and headed to the refrigerator to get a bottled water when I noticed she wrote her name and number down. I went and laid back in bed; my head was banging and still spinning. I tried going back to sleep until I heard my phone ringing and it was my son.

"What's up, JJ?" I asked, answering the phone.

"Hi Daddy, I miss you. Could you please come pick me up? Mommy said I can go with you." He giggled, dropping the phone. I heard his trifling ass mom in the background.

"Put your mom on the phone JJ." I snickered at his silly but.

"Okay, Daddy, I'll see you later." He handed his mom the phone.

"What, Pierre?" She popped her lips.

"Damn, hi to you too. Please have JJ ready. I'll be there to get him later on. I have to handle some shit first." I hung the phone up in her face and sat back down.

Chapter Five
SNOW

Three weeks later

It'd been three weeks since I last saw Pierre. He still hadn't called or text me. I was starting to feel stupid, real stupid losing my virginity to a nigga I didn't know. I looked through my emails when I noticed Desari sent me an invitation to the Flats hotels. I huffed and clicked on the link. I figured my brothers had something up their sleeves so I decided to text Desari.

Me: What is this invitation for?

Dezzy: Just show up, please. I promise you won't be disappointed, Snow. I love you, talk to you later.

Me: Okay!

I thought I would get somewhere texting her about the invite, but I didn't. I cleared my computer and was pulling files out of my bag when Pierre barged into my office with Lysa on his ass. I thought I was seeing shit but it was him in the flesh.

"Lysa, you know I only take people by appointments, not walk-ins," I stated, and rolled my eyes at her and Pierre.

"I'm sorry, Ms. Blacc, but he forced his way in here. I tried stopping him but he was being rude. Please don't be mad at me," she exclaimed, standing by the door with a dumb look on her face.

I looked up at Pierre, dismissing Lysa. She was so red and had tears running down her face that

I felt bad for talking to her like that. I made a mental note to talk to her before the end of the day.

"So, what made you stop by after three weeks?" I barked at him, getting up from my desk. I walked towards my meeting space in my office. I couldn't even front; he was looking good as hell but I couldn't look him in his eyes. Being pissed off was an understatement. I got talked out of my panties and played all in the same night.

"I knew I owed you a visit instead of a phone call."

I sighed. "Have a seat, Pierre." I sat across from him waiting on him to explain his actions.

"I know I haven't talk to you since that night and I'm sorry. I been dealing with a lot of shit and I didn't want to drag you into my messy ass life. I know I have a reputation with one-night stands, but it wasn't supposed to be like that with you," he

mumbled, getting up from his seat, walking around the table to sit next to me.

"You have to believe me, Snow. I'm sorry," he babbled.

My inner bitch was getting ready to come out and I tried my hardest to keep her under wraps. I took a couple seconds before speaking my mind. It took everything in me not to show my ass. I looked him in his eyes and saw some truth, but I also saw bullshit too. I just prayed to God he wasn't trying to play me because shit would get hectic fast.

"Look, Pierre… I really like you and it scares me a little bit that I like you. I had sex with you and that was my first time. I gave a special part of me away to you so please don't sit up here playing with my emotions."

"I said I was sorry, Snow, and it won't happen again. Have dinner with me tonight at Erre's steak house, please," he begged, getting on his knee.

It was a corny move but it was cute so I took him up on his offer.

"Yes, I'll go," I chimed while blushing.

"Good, text me your address." He kissed me on the lips and headed for the door.

I walked back to my office in a better mood. I called Lysa into my office so I could apologize for talking to her crazy. I had been hard on her since I hired her. I saw potential in her and I wanted her to be her best. She was young with a good head on her shoulders. I buzzed the intercom calling Lysa.

"Lysa, could you please come into my office," I said in a slightly calm tone.

Lysa came walking into my office looking scared. She was starting to turn red in the face. I noticed when she got emotional, her face turned different colors. I had to speak up. I didn't want her to think she was in trouble.

"You don't have to be on edge, Lysa, calm down and have a seat. I know lately I've been a bitch to you and I'm sorry. Around the holidays I get a little stressed out and act like the Grinch who stole Christmas. I've been through some horrible shit as a kid so Christmas is not an ideal holiday for me and I'm sorry for talking to you like that a few weeks ago and today. You are a human being just like me and you need to be respected as one, please forgive me," I uttered with a slight smile.

She sat there looking at me like I was a crazy person. She tried to read me and I knew exactly what she was doing. I realized Lysa was a pretty woman. She was a happy, emotional person. I pulled my skirt down and crossed my legs, waiting on her to say something.

"Thank you, Ms. Blacc. I know sometimes I can come off as a pushover, but I'm not. I love my job and I have the utmost respect for you. I would never do anything to jeopardize my job." She

grinned at me. She started crying until I stopped
her.

"Stop apologizing so much, Lysa, you didn't
do anything wrong," I snarled. "You are good
peoples and I see that. I'm not a fan of Christmas or
decorations but I have no right to strip that from you
or your belief. I got invited to an event for Saturday
and I want you to come with me if you didn't have
any plans." I gave her a sincere smile.

"I'm free Saturday night," she said excitedly,
getting up from my desk, walking out of the room,
leaving me to think about Pierre and our date
tonight.

I couldn't believe I was going on a date. If
my mom was here she would be happy. She said I
was a mean little girl growing up and that I'd never
have a boyfriend, now here I was dating and finally
lost my virginity.

I decided to leave work and go look for an outfit. It was wintertime so I needed to look cute and stay warm at the same damn time. I called for my driver and waited until he got there before leaving out the building.

Later that evening
SNOW

Erre's Steakhouse

We pulled up to the restaurant and it was
nice. It took me by surprise that Pierre knew about
this place; it was upscale. We walked in and the
place was empty. He had a table in the middle of the
restaurant with candles lighting up the whole place.
It was romantic; I didn't want to kill the vibe by
asking so many questions so I just smiled at his
sexy ass. Pierre was looking like everything in his
white and gold True Religion outfit. You could tell

he had just got a fresh line up. I licked my lips thinking of the things I could do to him.

He pulled my chair out from the table and I sat down then he took his seat. He whispered something into the chef's ear and he walked off towards the kitchen and came back with a nice bottle of Dom Perignon champagne. I couldn't help but smile.

"So, what's this all about, Mr. Pierre?" I asked, raising an eyebrow at him waiting on him to respond to me.

He cocked his head to the side and smirked at me.

"I told you I'm trying to make up for how I handled our situation," he stated, pouring wine into our glasses.

"Snow, what do you think I do for a living?" he asked, sitting the bottle of wine into a bucket of ice on the table.

"I don't know, a construction worker or something?" I answered truthfully. He looked at me and started laughing like I said some funny shit.

"I'm a business man… I own a few grocery stores, a few stocks and bonds, and I also own this restaurant we're sitting in right now," he explained, calling for the waiter to come to our table. I sat there listening to his words as they danced off his tongue. This man was so charming and well-spoken to be a hood nigga. It was scary in a sense, but I was enjoying it.

"I like you, Snow, and I know it might sound crazy so soon, but a nigga genuinely loves you. You gave me something so special. I felt like shit when I didn't call you after. When I came to your office earlier, I had to swallow my pride and come see you. If I was the first nigga to ever go up in you then I'm going to be the last," he blurted out, catching me way off guard. I choked on my wine because I thought I was hearing shit.

I excused myself and went to the bathroom. I stood there looking at myself in the mirror analyzing my body. I looked bloated in my outfit, and I knew my period was near because I was cramping. I then thought about what Pierre said to me. He wanted to be my last. Was he trying to say he wanted to marry me? I bitched up at the table and I was a little embarrassed now, but I knew I had to go back out there and face him. I splashed water on my face and then re-did my makeup. As I was walking up to the table I noticed it was covered in food and it smelled delicious. My mouth started watering at the sight of it.

"Are you okay, Snow?" Pierre asked as soon as I sat down.

"Yes, I'm okay."

He raised his eyebrow, and I gave him a smile.

"I promise I'm okay."

We ate dinner, talked and laughed. I was enjoying myself; I didn't want the night to end at all so we went back to Pierre's penthouse.

For him to be single he lived nice and it was clean. Most single niggas shit be looking like a trap house. He gave me a grand tour of the place and I fell in love. He must have sensed it too because he took me to his bedroom and it was just as nice. His room was painted a deep, smoky grey with white trim all around it.

"This is nice, Pierre," I said sitting on his fluffy bed.

He was standing by his dresser taking his jewelry off. He was well put together and organized. He told me to make myself at home, so I did. I got up and went into his bathroom. I turned on his glass shower then stepped in. As I washed my body, I saw Pierre standing there watching my every move. I tried to be sexy and it was an epic fail, I almost slipped. He ended up getting in with me and I didn't know how to feel.

"What you doing, Pierre?" I turned around to face him.

"Relax, Snow, I'm joining you if that's okay." He smirked while looking down at me.

Pierre kissed me, and I didn't resist him. My breathing picked up as he slipped a finger into my hot, wet box. He was driving me crazy. I couldn't stop the moans from escaping from my lips. Pierre sat me down on the bench in the shower, opening my legs, devouring me like I was his last meal he'd ever eat.

We explored each other's bodies for what seemed like hours in that shower. I felt weak, I was scared to stand up, all feeling in my legs were gone. Pierre picked me up off the shower bench and walked me into his room. He dried me off and laid my naked body on his bed. I couldn't help but stare at his sexy ass. For a change, I wanted to please him so I made him lay down.

"Lay down, Pierre, let me please you now."

I licked my lips and dropped to my knees while looking at his rock-hard dick. I didn't know how to suck dick but I was going to give it a try. I took him into my warm mouth. I tried to suck his dick but it was too wide and long. He must have sensed I didn't know what I was doing so he sat up.

"Snow, I know you probably doing this because you feel like you owe me, and you don't. I can teach you to suck my dick, Ma. Just relax and open your mouth. I'm going to stand up so you can get a better feel of me," he professed standing up.

A bitch's heart dropped. Not only was I fucking now, but I was sucking dick. I had all types of crazy thoughts going through my mind when Pierre told me what to do. I was all the way turned on. I was slowly starting to turn into a freak and if my dick sucking skills got better I was going to show out on his ass.

Pierre fucked me into a sleeping coma. I woke up the next morning sore as hell and with my head hurting. I smelled food being cooked so I got up to head to the kitchen to see what was being cooked. Upon walking into the kitchen, Pierre was cooking ass naked as the day he was born. I stood there looking at his sexy ass. I didn't say anything for at least three minutes watching him cut up in the middle of the kitchen.

"Well good morning to you, Pierre," I cheerfully said. I sat down at the island in the middle of the kitchen.

"Good morning, Snow, a nigga made you breakfast. It's nothing fancy but it's good," he proclaimed, sitting a plate of food down in front of me.

I sat there looking around his kitchen trying to avoid eye contact. After last night's festivities I didn't know how to act around him. He was starting to turn me out. When my eyes landed on him he was staring hard as hell at me and that bothered me.

"Why are you looking at me like that, Pierre?" I asked, sitting all the way up on the stool.

"You know you're my woman now, right?" he asked, getting up putting his plate into the dishwasher.

I had to double look at him. "I'm your what?" I asked in a serious tone.

"You heard me, Ma. After taking your virginity and the shit we did last night, I made you my woman."

"Well since I'm your woman now, I need for you to go to a family event with me Saturday if you're not busy," I said like a shy schoolgirl. "My brother is up to something and I'm going but it will be even better with you there with me."

"I'll go on one condition. If you allow me to take you shopping for your birthday." Pierre kissed me on the lips.

I wasn't going to argue with a free shopping trip. "Of course, Pierre. You can take me shopping."

After breakfast, Pierre took me home so I could get ready for work. I wanted to stay in and rest after my night with Pierre but I had a first-degree murder case on my hands and I needed to focus. It was something about her case that didn't sit with me too well. I hated seeing young black people in trouble. The justice system wasn't built for us. The day flew by quickly and I was dying to get in bed. I packed my briefcase up and turned off my computer and lights before heading out of my office.

As I left out, I ran into my brother Paul sitting there talking to Lysa.

"What are you doing here, Paul?" I asked raising an eyebrow, looking at him and Lysa.

"Dang, I'm chilling, Snow," he smacked his lips. He then got up from his seat and grabbed my bag.

"Have a good night, Lysa." I waved at her getting into the elevator, glaring at Paul. He never stopped by my office like that before so it was suspicious to me, but I minded my own business. Instead of calling for my driver, Paul took me home.

"You didn't have to do this, Paul. I know you had other plans," I spoke, looking over at him driving.

"Yes, I do. I feel like we need to get reconnected, so picking you up from work unexpectedly is a start."

"You know you were always my fav even though Aaron took care of us," I expressed with a smile.

I got to my house and cooked us some dinner. Paul told me he had a crush on Lysa and I thought it was the cutest thing. My brother was a grown man now so I didn't say anything out the way to make him uncomfortable.

"You just better make sure she don't get distracted from her work while on the job but if Lysa makes you happy go for it, bro." I gave him my blessing to date Lysa.

After we finished eating, Paul left. I then went to my office after I straightened up my kitchen. I pulled out my files and went over them. That's when I noticed this young lady had a Personal Protection Order out on her baby father at the time the murder occurred. I made sure to write reminder notes for Monday morning in court. After looking deeper into her cases, I found out he was also her stepfather. I got up from my desk making a call to the Kent County Correctional Center letting them know I'd be in first thing tomorrow morning.

SNOW

I got up early Saturday morning so I could meet with this young lady about her case. If she was found not guilty she would be free and it would be good for business; my ranking would go all the way up. I decided to drive myself. I started my car up before leaving out the house so it could be warm. I made sure I had all my paperwork. When I arrived to the jail it was like a ghost town in the parking lot. My phone started ringing so I answered it without looking at the caller ID.

"Hello," I answered, my tone rude.

"Damn, queen, what's wrong with you?" Pierre asked, sounding concerned.

"I'm okay, I'm getting ready to see a client right now and she needs my full, undivided attention. I don't have time to talk right now, I'm sorry. I'll call you when I get free time today."

"Okay, well call me when you are done. I'm about to go get my son and take him shopping," Pierre said before hanging up.

As I walked up to the jail, I saw how small the windows were. They looked like caged animals.

I checked in so I could meet with my client. They took forever bringing her down to see me and it pissed me off.

"Hello, good afternoon, Ms. Palmer. I'm your lawyer, Ms. Blacc. I needed to meet with you about your case. There were some things that stuck out to me in your file. You had a baby by your stepfather? And he beat you? I see you put a protective order on him a while back."

She looked at me with tears in her eyes.

"Yes, he had been raping me since I was twelve. After I had my baby and turned eighteen, I tried to get away from him but he kept following me. He showed up at my house in the middle of the night. He kicked the door in looking for me. I asked him to leave but he wouldn't leave so I called the police and he went crazy, choking me. I grabbed a knife and stabbed him and I been here since." She broke down crying.

I felt bad for her. I went over her case letting her know what to expect come Monday morning. I left out of the jail all emotional. I needed to go home and relax. So that's what I did. I knew Pierre was going to be mad I didn't call him back but my job was stressful at times to the point I needed to be alone.

Chapter Six
LUKE...

I laid in a penthouse suite I had been living in for weeks with two of the finest bitches I brought back from the club last night. They were down for whatever and I was down too. After I left Pierre's goons, I went to release some much-needed stress. My nephew had these little niggas thinking they were running shit and they wasn't. Pierre was too trusting with these niggas, and that didn't sit too well with me. I didn't like the way he was handling the situation with Aaron Jr. and my name was buzzing about killing Aaron Blacc over my fifty grand. All Pierre did was bark orders, but I was the one doing all the biting.

I got out the bed and headed into the living room area. I tripped over heels and purses as I made my way to find my phone. I had a wild ass night. Hell, I didn't know how we got back to my suite. I went to make room on the couch when I noticed it was some coke left over on the table. I did two lines before making my call. I called Pierre's long-lost brother Shawn. On the third ring I was getting ready to hang up until he picked up.

"Yo, what the fuck you want?" the voice boomed through the speaker. Music was playing in the background.

I was getting close with this nigga Shawn. He wasn't like his hoe ass brother Pierre. He had what it took to run the game, but his mouth was too reckless when he spoke to me. Shawn and Pierre didn't even know they're brothers. Shawn's mom was a hoe, so my brother Pierre Sr. never wifed her. I ended up with her, and our relationship failed too.

"Don't ever talk to me like that again, blood. I'm trying to help you take over an empire so chill the fuck out," I yelled at my nephew through the phone, then I continued, "Look, Pierre having a Christmas dinner tomorrow night and I need for you to be there. He needs to look the next boss nigga in his face and meet the long-lost brother he never had but wished for growing up. I'll hit you with the whereabouts later on," I barked at him, but I knew he wasn't listening since he cut me off in mid-sentence.

"Don't call me barking orders, nigga. You don't run shit but your mouth, nigga," Shawn hollered, hanging up in my face.

I got up off the couch when I heard one of them hoe's feet hit the floor. I walked in the room as she was going through my damn pockets. I smacked her pretty, high yellow ass to the floor and snatched her by her hair.

"Bitch, don't ever in your life go through my fucking pockets," I barked, throwing her to the floor, smacking the other bitch up out my bed. This shit never seems to amaze me; these bitches were getting bold as fuck out here now. She started crying but it didn't faze me.

"I told you bitches to not go through my shit now look what the fuck your rat ass doing. Get the fuck up out my shit before y'all be some dead bitches." I kicked her in the stomach. The girl with the blonde hair got out of the bed, speaking up.

"We not going anywhere until you pay us for our services or shit is going to get real messy and fast," she spat putting her clothes back on.

These hoes were starting to get out of pocket talking to me crazy.

"Y'all must not know who the fuck I am," I barked at them, but they didn't look bothered at all. Baby girl with the blonde hair and fat ass screamed at me.

"We don't give a fuck who you are! Pay up or get fucked up, it doesn't matter which one you pick, nigga." She sat down on the edge of my bed. She pulled a phone out and made a call.

"Hello, yeah, this nigga trying not to pay us!" she yelled into the phone.

I was tired of going back and forth with these bitches. The coke I had snorted had me on one, so I walked to the nightstand in the corner of my room. I pulled my gun out and shot baby girl on the floor in the head. Before the blonde bitch could react, I popped her ass too. These hoes was going to learn the hard way. I had to meet with someone, so I left them where they dropped.

I had shit to handle and them hoes was holding me up. I walked out of the hotel like shit was normal and it wasn't. I had one thing on my mind and that was getting to the money and taking over the streets of Grand Rapids.

WHO IS SHAWN...

Growing up, I had it hard. My mother was a crack whore and my daddy didn't gave a damn about me so I ended up in the system. When I turned eighteen, I got a hold of my file and found out I had a father, his name was Pierre Mathen. He lived in Michigan his whole life and never tried to get me out the system.

One day I took it upon myself and made a visit to his house. He answered the door not recognizing who I was, and that shit hurt. I told him who my mother was and that I was his son. He told me his wife made him pick and he choose her over us. He gave me $1,000 and sent me on my way, telling me to never show back up at his house again. Since that day forward I hated that nigga.

I made my own way living in the streets. When I found out he had a son named after him I was hot. I wanted him dead. I found out Luke was my uncle and he took me in. By that time though, I was too deep in the streets and there was no bringing me back.

When I found out he died, the shit didn't even hurt. He left Pierre Jr. everything, and I was coming for everything that little high yellow nigga had and I was going to get it by any means necessary. My momma died because of Pierre Sr. He got her strung out on heroin. Pierre whole empire was about to come crumbling down.

Snow Blacc   Ruby

Chapter Seven
SNOW'S SURPISE PARTY...

Lysa and Pierre walked me into a building blindfolded. I was nervous as hell because I invited them out with me and they kidnapped me somehow. Lysa finally took the blindfold off me and we stood in front of a red door. I felt sick all over again seeing the Christmas decorations plastered everywhere. I opened the door and got the shock of my life. It was all seven of my brothers standing there with a dozen red roses in each of their hands. I was in shock as they all yelled, "Happy birthday!" Even Lysa and Pierre yelled it. I was so busy trying to forget about Christmas that I almost forgot about my own birthday being a couple days before Christmas.

I walked into the ballroom and the DJ started playing my favorite song "Step in the Name of Love" by R. Kelly. We all danced, talked, and laughed. Aaron even hired a photographer to capture the whole night. It was flash after flash; I was enjoying myself.

Aaron tapped his glass with a butter knife and the music was instantly cut. Aaron and Desari stood at the head of the table and gave a speech while a slideshow of pictures played on a projector behind him. I took in every word he said.

After Aaron and his wife made their speeches, all of my brothers stood up giving their own little speech making me emotional.

"Snow, I know it's been rocky, baby girl, but your time is coming," Marcus spoke, and then passed the microphone to Devon.

Drew, Nico, Peter, and Paul stood to their feet while Devon talked.

"It's been a long eight years, sis, and we're glad to have you back in our lives, Lady Blacc," my brother Nico expressed. He was the meanest of all my brothers. He would play pranks on me to the point I couldn't sleep at night sometimes. So to hear him say what he said to me made me feel good.

"We love you and happy birthday," all of my brothers said in unison.

After their speeches, we cried and laughed at some of the slides of us when we were kids that came across the projector. After our moment was over, I introduced Desari to Pierre. They started talking and hugged each other. I was lost until Desari spoke up.

"No need to introduce us, Snow, we already know each other. We're first cousins," Desari smiled.

"Say what now? You and Pierre are first cousins?" I asked, cocking my head looking at both of them. Desari and Pierre stood there smiling but I didn't see anything funny.

Out of nowhere, Aaron and Marcus came walking up on us at full speed. I just knew shit was getting ready to hit the fan. I prayed to God that this boy didn't show his ass in this party. Everybody started to look at us and I already didn't want to celebrate my birthday. Typical Aaron had to show his ass…

Chapter Eight
THE SEVEN THUGS: AARON...

I saw my wife hugging that nigga Pierre and all I saw was blood. He was a dead nigga for being all up on my woman like that; everybody knew she was off fucking limits. When Marcus pointed the shit out to me it pissed me off instantly. When I saw Snow with him, I had to play it cool because I didn't want to ruin her birthday when she already hated celebrating it. That nigga was bad for business and I needed to holler at him ASAP. I stopped talking to my brothers, walking towards Snow and them. Snow must have sensed I was pissed off because her facial expression said it all. I walked up on Desari ready to smack fire from her dumb ass.

"Yo, what the fuck is this shit?" I barked at my wife and Pierre. When I said that, Pierre turned around and his eyes landed on me.

"Yeah, pussy nigga, it's me," I barked at him, pulling my pistol from behind my back. "You thought you could come up in here and fuck on my wife? But this ain't that, my nigga." I cocked my gun letting everybody know I was 'bout to air this bitch out. Snow jumped in front of Pierre which pissed me off even more.

"Get the fuck out the way, Snow." I tried pushing her, but she was not budging.

Pierre moved Snow to the side and stepped in my face like he was getting ready to do some shit. Snow screamed at both of us but we didn't back down. It was about to be a *First 48* scene up in here if he didn't explain why he was hugging my wife, and he came to the party with Snow.

"Nigga, why the fuck are you here? I tried to play shit cool when I saw your ass walk through the door with my sister, since we in public. But you got shit fucked up hugging my wife, my nigga," I looked over at Snow who was hugging Pierre's arm tight. Desari tried to speak but I cut her ass off. I gave her ass the look of death. She folded her arms across her chest, showing off much attitude.

"If you stop acting so fucking crazy you would know Pierre is my first cousin," she blurted out smacking her lips, shifting from one leg to the other.

When she said that, everybody's heads turned.

My wife was family to my enemy? I was speechless.

For the first time I had my own foot in my mouth. I felt bad for going off on her like that in front of everyone, but I never knew they were family. My wife didn't talk to me the whole night and that fucked with a nigga's head. I had to sit my pride aside and apologize. The ride home was stale. She didn't even look at me. I pulled in the driveway and she tried to get out but I pulled her back in.

"I'm sorry, Desari, you know how I get with niggas being around you, especially if I don't know them or like them. How was I supposed to know Pierre was your cousin? He didn't come to the wedding or a family event so excuse me for going off. I don't like that nigga at all."

Desari sat there hearing me out but she never spoke. I knew she still had an attitude with me so I took the key out the ignition. I got out and slammed the door. I tried to apologize but I wasn't about to kiss her ass.

I opened the front door to our house and she stormed in walking past me, slamming her purse on the table in the hallway.

"You really want to know what my problem is, Aaron, huh?" she yelled, walking up on me. I tried to put my keys in the bowl on the table but she blocked me from doing that.

"Look Desari, I said I was sorry so please go on about your night. I'll sleep in the guest bedroom so you can cool off for the night. Just know I love you to death and I would never harm you." I tongue kissed her for a couple minutes before walking off, heading upstairs to the guest bedroom.

I took a hot shower so I could wash the crazy night off of me. I brushed my teeth and headed back into the guest room when I walked in seeing Desari naked sitting on her knees in the middle of the bed.

"What you doing in here, girl? I thought you was mad at a nigga. Now you want some dick so you're being nice," I asked, snatching my towel off laying in the bed.

"Look, Aaron, you are my husband. I could never stay mad at you but you really need to check yourself. You are getting too old to keep acting like a teenager. I'm scared to lose you to the streets or prison," she said, climbing on top of me. Her being next to me had always made me level headed.

I flipped her ass over on her stomach, easing my way into her pussy. She moaned out, gripping the sheets. I was fucking her long and hard. She screamed out her stomach hurt so I laid down making her reverse cowgirl on the dick. I pulled on her hair making her ass causing her to moan. After she came a few times it was time for me to get mine. I made her scoot to the edge of the bed and I went knee deep in her pussy. She started squirting on my dick and that made me go crazy. She tried running but I grabbed her by her hips, pounding her shit until I came. My toes curled and cracked; that was a well-needed nut. We both were out of breath breathing heavy. Desari got up to clean herself and got a warm washcloth for me, cleaning me up.

"I love you, Aaron," she whispered in my ear before I drifted off to sleep.

Chapter Nine
PIERRE

Shit happened so fast at Snow's party, it took everybody by surprise. My enemy was basically family. I wasn't expecting to see Desari there with Aaron. We hadn't seen each other in years. So I understood why everybody was surprised. I felt like a piece of meat in a lion's den but I held my own weight. Aaron pulled the strap out on me and shit got real. Snow took off crying and it was a lot of yelling between their family members. I didn't like that Desari knuckled under that nigga Aaron either. My pride wouldn't let me back down and go after Snow, but I wasn't letting Aaron and his brothers hoe me either, that was a no go for me. I was my own nigga, I made my own rules, and rule number one was to never be scared of the next nigga.

"Look, Aaron, with all due respect, my nigga… don't pull a gun out on me unless you're going to use it," I spat clinching my jaws.

Desari stepped in the middle of us explaining to her husband that we were family but he wasn't trying to hear shit she was saying. When he pushed me, I flipped out, but Snow ran over to us screaming and crying.

"Stop it, stop it! What the fuck is going on with y'all two? Y'all know each other or something?" she yelled, looking at both of us with tears in her eyes, her makeup ruined. Snow went to sit down when Aaron started to break shit down to her.

"Snow, this is the nigga I've been beefing with the last few months about some shit you don't need to worry about," Aaron admitted.

Snow looked confused and hurt, but I had no idea she was Aaron's baby sister.

"You played me, Pierre, to get close to my brother. You knew who I was this whole time, huh?" she snapped, leaving out of the ballroom with Desari and Lysa following after her.

I felt like shit; I had ruined Snow's party. I left out of the ballroom trying to find Snow, but she was nowhere to be found. I tried calling her and she sent me to voicemail.

"Fuck!" I shouted, throwing my phone at the wall breaking it. I had to find her so we could talk. I walked down Monroe looking for her; it was cold and dark. Downtown was not a place for a woman to be alone at night. I walked to the Rosa Parks

Center finding her and the girls sitting at a table talking and freezing.

"Desari, Aaron is looking for you." I grabbed a chair sitting in front of Snow. Desari and Lys got up, leaving me and Snow to talk.

"I didn't know the Blacc boys were your brothers. I swear to God, you have to believe me," I groaned.

"I believe you, Pierre, thanks to Desari. She told me you wouldn't get down like that." She smiled at me.

"Look, your brother Aaron is a hot head in these streets and I am too. There's some things I didn't tell you but now that it's out here, I promise I won't ever put you in harm's way. I don't know where things are going to go now that I know we are damn near family, but I promise I won't interfere with you. I'm sorry for messing up your party." I gave her a sincere look.

"It's okay. I don't know why they do these things for me. I don't like Christmas as it is. Who would like the day their parents were murdered?" I sat next to her and wrapped my jacket around her freezing arms.

I didn't want to dig deep into why she didn't like Christmas so I sat silent.

"I think we should head back. I think it's best you wait for me in the car while I say my goodbyes."

I helped Snow from the bench and we headed back to the venue. I sat in my car smoking a blunt, thinking about what had went down. Aaron was a lucky man tonight because putting a gun to my face always cost a nigga his life.

LUKE

I met up with Pierre's supplier trying to get shit back on track, but I knew it wouldn't be easy trying to take over. Pierre was not letting me take over without a fight and that fight I was prepared for. I had recruited my own niggas because if I had to go to war with my nephew then so be it.

I hated dealing with these taco eating muthafuckas. They took their time every time when we met up. Ricardo finally pulled up. Me and Shawn exited the car ready for whatever.

"What's this, papi? Who is this nigga?" Ricardo asked, signaling his boys to search us, taking our guns from us.

"This is Shawn, Pierre's older brother. He will be taking over very shortly," I mumbled, sitting the money on the hood of the car so his workers could make sure all the money was there. Ricardo looked at me telling me what he expected from me, but I wasn't tripping. I was Luke, I'm the man in the streets.

"I don't know what you and Pierre have going on, Luke, but I'm going to tell you like this… I need all my money by New Years. If I don't have it by then, it's your ass." He grabbed me by the neck meaning every word. His workers threw the black duffle bags to the ground.

Snow Blacc   Ruby

After we put the shit in the car, we left from dealing with Ricardo. I had one last stop to make to drop this shit off at the trap house. Pierre was throwing Christmas dinner and I was taking Shawn with me. I wanted to see the look on Pierre's face when he found out he wasn't his father's only son. I got a kick out of seeing this nigga always being mad when shit didn't go his way.

Upon arriving to his party, I saw a pretty little chocolate thang and her girlfriends get out of a Lyft. I was going to talk to her by the end of the night.

When she walked through the door all eyes were on her. As she got closer, I noticed it was Snow, Aaron Sr.'s daughter, but I brushed it off. She probably didn't remember me anyway. I bumped into her in the hallway and she didn't say anything. I kept on going about my business until an hour later when Aaron Jr. walked through the door…

Snow Blacc   Ruby

Chapter Eleven

PIERRE'S DINNER PARTY: SNOW

I got an invitation to Pierre's holiday dinner so I took it upon myself to invite Desari and Lysa. I needed the support; they knew how I felt about Christmas and I needed them there with me. We walked up in his house like the boss bitches we were. All eyes were on us and I knew Lysa's single ass was loving every bit of it.

This boy Pierre went all out. He even had servers and shit; he outdid himself. I took a glass of bubbly looking around for Pierre when my eyes landed on him. I instantly got wet, he was fine as hell. I had to use the bathroom so I excused myself from talking to the ladies.

I walked down the hallway trying to find the bathroom.

"I'm sorry, Sir, didn't see you there," I politely told him, stepping to the side letting him leave out the bathroom.

"You're okay, Ms. Snow. Have a good night," he replied as he walked down the hallway back to the party. It dawned on me that I never gave him my name, that's when I saw red flags. I needed to find Pierre fast because something didn't feel right.

After I used the bathroom and washed my hands, I went looking for Pierre. I saw him, Desari, and Lysa talking and laughing with each other so I decided to play it cool like I wasn't bothered. But I definitely was going to ask Pierre who the man was.

When I finally made it to him the server rang the bell for dinner letting us know it was time to start. His whole house was beautiful and the setup of the dinner was too. We were all seated in assigned areas of the table. Pierre and I sat next to each other and the man from the hallway sat across from me. As we sat sipping champagne waiting for the food to come from the kitchen, the man from the hallway just kept looking at me.

"Pierre, who is this sitting across from us staring at me?" I whispered in his ear, not breaking eye contact with the stranger across from me. He had bad energy and I didn't like it at all.

"That's my uncle Luke; he's my daddy's older brother. He's a weirdo like that," Pierre truthfully told me.

That's when it hit me who the man was. I had lost my appetite. I remembered seeing him the night before my parents died and I always thought he had something to do with my parents' deaths. I didn't say a word though because I didn't want to ruin Pierre's party with his family but I definitely wasn't staying. I got up from the table and walked onto the balcony to get some fresh air. I called Aaron, asking him if he could come get us. I was no longer in the mood to celebrate anything with a man that could have possibly killed my parents.

I finally made my way back into the dinner party when I heard the doorbell. I knew it was Aaron because he didn't live far from Pierre. Upon walking into the house, I sensed tension in the room. I had a feeling all hell was about to break loose. Aaron walked in with my other brother mean mugging everybody. When his eyes landed on Luke, shots were fired. I dropped to the floor screaming, hoping I didn't get hit with a bullet. I looked up and Luke and some weird looking guy were shooting. I was lost until I heard Aaron clear as day yelling.

"Get my sister and wife up out of here now!" he barked, running after Luke.

I was picked up off the floor. I kicked and screamed until I saw Paul and Peter walking with Desari and Lysa out of the house. Once all of us were in the truck, they took off leaving us in the backseat terrified.

"What the fuck was that about?" Lysa asked while still sobbing and shaking.

"I don't know but whatever just happened in there it's not good." I wiped my tears away.

We ended up at Aaron and Desari's house. Paul and Peter weren't letting us up out of their sight. We sat on the couch trying to figure out what happened. I laid down on the couch because my anxiety was at an all-time high. I laid there thinking about Pierre. Did he know that would happen? The suspense was driving me crazy. I grabbed my cellphone and texted Pierre.

Me: What the fuck, Pierre?

Pierre: Snow, I don't know what's going on. Let me hit you back, please.

Me: You played me, you knew about my parents this whole time?

Pierre: What? I don't know anything about your parents!

Me: Bye, Pierre, I don't want to talk to you until I get to the bottom of this.

I felt so stupid all over again. There was no way Pierre didn't know about Luke knowing my father. I felt he knew who killed my parents and that's why him and Aaron were really beefing, but nobody wanted to tell me the truth.

I was ready to go home and get in bed; I was over the night at hand. Lysa probably thought my family was crazy. Every time some shit went down my brothers were always in the middle of it. Since

the twins didn't take me home I went to one of
Aaron's spare bedrooms and locked myself in the
room for the rest of the night. It was so hard trying
to fall asleep. I wanted to lay in my bed but my
brothers were being strict; none of us could leave
the house. I ignored Pierre's calls and text messages
until I fell asleep.

LUKE

I stood in front of Pierre's house blowing
smoke from my ears because I was so livid. He was
pissed I shot up his dinner party in front of family,
and I didn't care. I wanted Aaron's head, and now I
really wanted to knock Pierre off the map and let
Shawn take over. I was tired of this little nigga
thinking he ran shit. If he wanted to cut me off
because of some pussy and a bitch ass nigga, he had
another thing coming. I knew he wasn't going to
back down and neither was I. I punched him in the
face causing him to stumble back a little. He spit

blood out of his mouth, wiped it and swung back. I could see his little niggas were ready to pull the trigger but I wasn't dumb enough to come on my own. I had my niggas with me ready to pop a pussy nigga.

"All this over some enemies?" I spat, ducking one of his punches. "You want to do this all because this hoe said I killed her parents. You sure I didn't fuck her and her feelings just hurt? I don't even know who that bitch is, my nigga," I barked. I tackled Pierre and knocked him to the ground. I could tell I hit a nerve with that one.

Everybody broke us up and we stood to our feet when I noticed he had a gun pointed at me.

"Let me tell you something, young blood, don't' pull a gun out and not use it. That's what's wrong with you young, dumb muthafuckas. You really about to kill me over this bitch and her brothers? Fuck you, Pierre, and you better hope them bullets kill me. If not, nigga, you are going to have a rude awakening," I growled at Pierre, letting him know I wasn't scared of him.

"I don't want you to fear me, nigga, but you will know I'm not that nigga to be fucked with. I'll see you when I see you, nigga." Pierre walked off like he had just won the championship.

"You a dead nigga walking, Pierre. Dead nigga." I spat blood from my mouth. "Let's get the fuck up out of here." I looked at my niggas with blood on my white tee.

"His days are numbered, mark my words," I blurted out, snatching my gun from one of my goons. That nigga Pierre was a pain in my ass and I couldn't wait to kill him.

Shawn called me asking how the meeting went, just to piss me off.

"Listen here, blood, you never show the right hand what the left hand doing." I hung up in his face for once. I went to the trap to see if Shawn and the boys started bagging up that work.

I got pissed off when I pulled up to the trap. These niggas was having a fucking house party when they were supposed to be cooking up dope and bagging it. I walked in cutting the music off.

"Where the fuck is Shawn at?" I barked at his dumb ass friends. They all shrugged their shoulders acting like they didn't know where he was.

I walked through the house looking for this nigga. I found him in the kitchen with three bitches naked while chopping up dope.

"What the fuck is this, Shawn? You having a party while niggas supposed to be working?" I scoffed at him, putting my hands in my pocket because I really wanted to pistol whip his dumb ass.

"Everybody get the fuck out before I air this bitch out now," I demanded, clearing the house out.

When I pulled my gun out niggas and the bitches put a pep in their steps.

After making sure the house was empty, I let Shawn have it.

"Nigga, don't you ever in your life do some dumb ass shit like that again or we gon' have a problem," I barked at him, not taking my eyes off the three hoes. They looked scared because the bass in my voice was bold and deep, but I didn't give a fuck. This nigga was trying to take over an empire and was making rookie mistakes like throwing house parties. My life was on the line for this careless ass nigga, so I was ready to murder his ass, especially after just fighting his brother...

Chapter Thirteen

THE SEVEN THUGS: AARON

My brothers sat in the living room while I handled business with our connect in Mexico over the phone. After I had left with my family at the dinner party, Pierre called me and told me he wasn't the one shooting and it was Luke shooting at me. That made me see shit a whole lot different now. He told me he and Luke were now enemies and he wanted to meet with me to talk about what had happened. I knew me and Pierre had beef in the streets over dirty money, and put blood on the streets from our goons, but this shit with Luke was on another level. He killed my parents, now he wants me dead? He was shooting at parties and shit; that shit wasn't cool. Pierre walked into my den looking tired. After confirming everything, he was allowed in my home and around my brothers. Plus the nigga loved my sister to death so I respected that. But I had to get down on the deal with Luke, and I knew Pierre was going to open up to me on whatever he knew.

"What's up, Aaron?" Pierre asked as he sat down on the love seat I had in my office. He laid his head back and put his hand over his face. He took a deep breath before exhaling.

I was rolling a blunt while on the phone talking. I needed to ease my mind after the shit that happened at his holiday dinner. This shit with Luke was out of hand. People could have lost their lives last night at Pierre's dinner party. Snow called me freaking out that night and I showed up to see what she was so uncomfortable about. She said it was a man there that made her feel uneasy so I did what I do best, popped up on a nigga to see what the deal was. When I got there, it was Luke. It surprised me Snow remembered Luke from that night eight years ago. After that, the nigga started shooting as soon as we made eye contact.

I got up from my office desk and walked around it. I sat in a chair in front of Pierre so I could explain why I came to his house like I had done.

"I know Luke is your uncle, but he killed my parents eight years ago, bro. Snow felt unsafe so she called me to come get her and the girls. I didn't tell her Luke was the killer, but she has this thing with energy, and Luke's was off. Plus, she remembered the nigga from the night before my folks were killed. When my baby sister calls me frantic like that, I show up with no questions asked. I wasn't expecting for Luke to get ignorant in a house full of people and start shooting up a dinner party. But I should have known because word was out I was on his head." I sat back sparking my blunt, letting the smoke fill my lungs. Pierre felt where I was coming from, he didn't even argue with me.

"This nigga Luke has to go ASAP. I don't care how he leaves this earth but he has to go. He tried to kill both of us, and now that me and him fought right after the party, he wants my head." Pierre got up, pacing the floor back and forth.

"We will get him just let me know when you ready." I got up from my seat walking out of my office headed back into the living room with my brothers so we could finish talking about our business. We had a huge shipment coming in within the next week and I needed them niggas to be on ten toes just in case anything happened.

After Pierre left, my brothers were looking at me crazy. They wanted to know what happened so I told them what the deal was. They were skeptical but they went with my flow because they knew I wouldn't lead them the wrong way.

Chapter Fourteen
PIERRE

I jumped out my truck creeping on Luke porch ready to catch a body. One of my niggas kicked his door in and we barged into his shit ready for war. When I walked into the living room, Luke was getting lit off our product. He always snorted up most of the dope in the trap house and complained about we were coming up short, but he was the reason. He had to go; this shit was ending real soon. It was one thing to try to kill me but he killed my girl's parents, and he knew the whole time who Snow and Aaron were. I felt like this nigga played me and I was done playing his fucking games. I was beefing with the brother and dating the sister that wasn't going to work out. Family or not, Luke had to go. Luke knew who Aaron was this whole time. He always had it out for Aaron more than me and now I knew why.

I pointed my gun at Luke and he looked up and smirked at me with dope on his nose.

"So you and this bitch nigga really gonna link up and take me out?" Luke gritted at me and Aaron as he eyed both of us.

"Nigga, you been having me beef with Aaron for no reason. All the while you been saying Aaron was the reason our money was short and it was you just trying to kill him because your secret hit the streets that you were the one who killed his parents!" I shouted at Luke.

"I was looking out for you, nigga. Had I not got y'all beefing your daddy's empire would have went to shits because I knew you would let this sucker ass nigga take over!" Luke shouted, but he had no clue what he was talking about.

Aaron's brother Marcus went into a back room to search the place and came back with a strange look on his face.

"What's wrong, what did you find?" Aaron asked. Marcus handed us some pictures and notes about the whole Blacc family. We also found a picture of a little boy, which threw all of us off.

"Yo, who is this little nigga?" Marcus asked Aaron because he wasn't one of their family members. I didn't know who it was either, but he looked real familiar to me.

"I've seen this nigga before I just can't remember where," I answered honestly. I then looked around the room. I looked at Aaron and his brothers. That's when I made eye contact with Paul and Peter. Peter started yelling get down. Bullets came crashing through the house hitting the pale, dirty walls. I saw Luke run to the back of the house but I couldn't even go after him because bullets were in the way.

"Lucky ass nigga," I mumbled as I got down on the floor.

"It's two trucks deep outside, my niggas, what the fuck we about to do?" Paul barked, crawling away from the door entrance.

I had to take charge, the bullets weren't stopping. I instructed everyone to split up in the house just in case they came inside. After having a shootout for about five minutes, we heard the front door open, and I heard Paul screaming he was hit in the leg. A tall nigga walked in the living room and that's when I remembered the boy from the picture we were just looking at. I jumped up, pointing my gun at him and he did the same. We were having a standoff.

"Nigga, do you know who the fuck I am?" I spat with spit flying from my mouth; furious was an understatement. I had fully turned into the devil, I was tired of my life being played with.

"Fuck you, pussy nigga, I know exactly who you are, Pierre. My daddy left my mother because of your hoe ass mom and we lost everything because of him. So it's time for you to lose, my nigga. Time's up, now your family can see what it's like to starve and loose everything," Shawn scolded raising his gun.

Aaron walked up behind Shawn and hit him in the back of the head, knocking him out cold. I stood there looking down at Shawn and his facial features, and he was indeed my brother. I had so many thoughts running through my head, I couldn't speak.

After dropping them other niggas outside like flies, we got the fuck up out of there before the police got there. Luke's bitch ass got away, but he was going to get got.

12 hours later
PIERRE

I punched my desk as hard as I could because I was angry that Luke's bitch ass got away. There was no coming back from what he had done; he was going to sleep with the fish. I couldn't give him another pass, especially after shooting at me and turning my brother I didn't know I had against me. I stood there yelling at every nigga in the warehouse, including Aaron's soldiers.

"We need that nigga Luke alive. We got twenty-grand on his head for whoever brings his ass in to us," I barked while looking at everybody so they knew I was serious.

"If you got eyes on him, stay on him until me and Aaron get there. I don't care where y'all at," I fumed, walking off.

Aaron followed me so we could talk in private. I felt funny about us working together now that I was with Snow and he was married to my cousin. We had no choice but to get along for their sake.

"Pierre, I know how we can get this nigga," Aaron stated, rubbing his hands together. "You know that old nigga thinks he's rich and stays in the club tricking with them young ass hoes. I know a few bitches that will lure him in our hands but you have to trust me, man. I know we've never seen eye to eye, but trust me on this one. I'm about to hit these hoes up and put the plan in motion," Aaron stated, and I liked how he was thinking.

"Aight, bet. Just let me know the time and place."

We shook hands on the deal.

Charistmas Eve

AARON

We sat outside of Sensations Strip Club waiting on the strippers to walk Luke's hoe ass out so we could capture him. When I saw Luke staggering out of the club, I laughed to myself... his dumb ass fell for the bait.

Pierre and I slid out the car and ran up on Luke. I hit him in the back of the head with the butt of my gun, causing him to fall to the ground. He started bleeding from his head.

"What the fuck, Pierre!" Luke shouted, not evening realizing I was the one that hit him. He felt the back of his head as blood poured out onto the cement. When he looked up and looked me in my eyes, all I saw was fear. He knew he had fucked up and there was no coming back from it. Just looking at him pissed me off.

"Oh, you scared, huh? You pussy ass nigga. Get the fuck up before I kill you and these hoes right here," I barked while grabbing him off the ground.

Pierre opened the trunk to the car and we tossed Luke's bitch ass in. We pulled out the parking lot and hit the gas. We called our goons up telling them to meet us at the spot. It was time to put this shit to rest so my parents could rest easy knowing their killer was no longer breathing.

After driving twenty minutes, we finally pulled into the dark parking lot. All our soldiers stood out there prepared to put in work. I saw my

six brothers jump out of Marcus' truck. We then
headed into the building with Luke's bitch ass
crying and begging for his life, but that shit went on
deaf ears. My brothers were ready to kill Luke but I
made my niggas lay plastic down because it was
going to get messy. We had Shawn locked in a dark
room. When Luke saw Shawn, he almost pissed
himself.

Pierre punched Shawn, causing him to fall.
Everybody in the room was silent, but Shawn
started mumbling under his breath.

"Please don't kill me, I was just doing what
I was told by Luke. He was trying to set y'all up
and have me take over the empire." He broke down
crying. Luke lunged at Shawn, telling him to shut
up, but Shawn opened his mouth spilling the news.

"I'm sorry, Pierre. I wish I could have been
a better brother and had a better relationship with
you. But your father dissed me at his door." He
dropped his head because he knew he fucked up.

"Nigga, you thought you could come for me and not get touched? This nigga Luke wasn't putting you on, he was using your dumb ass. You got so much hate for me for something our dad did, not me, that you let this nigga Luke fuck your life up," Pierre yelled, pulling his gun out, emptying the whole clip into Shawn. Brother or not, he didn't show him any mercy.

"Luke, you won't die so easily." I laughed at his scary ass. Now that Pierre got his revenge out the way, it was my turn.

"Put the nigga in the chair and chain him up. Me and my brothers got a real treat for this bitch ass nigga." I grinned at him.

My brothers beat his ass like they were lions. I let it go on for a good twenty minutes before I stepped in. He was bleeding bad and coughing up blood, but I was just getting started.

"One of you niggas hand me that chainsaw off the shelf," I demanded. I took off my jacket and put on gloves. I started the chainsaw up and Luke passed out.

"Throw some water on this nigga, I need him awake." I tapped one of my workers. Once he did, Luke woke up.

"You can sleep when you are dead, nigga, wake the fuck up. What you did will forever haunt us. My father trusted you. He let you in our house and you betrayed him. Now it's time for you to go, my nigga. Your time is up." I took the chainsaw and cut one of his hands off. His screaming was pissing me off.

"Find something to shut this nigga the fuck up!" I yelled out loud.

Pierre stuck a towel in his mouth and I went back to chopping on his ass. He passed out a few times from the pain; it was blood everywhere. I gave the chainsaw to Pierre so he could finish his hoe ass uncle up. Once Luke was dead, I called the cleaning crew up to clean Shawn and Luke up. It was late in the morning, and I needed to get home to my wife. She was going to be pissed.

"Boss man, where do you want us to put these niggas at?" one of my soldiers yelled out.

"Put they bitch asses in the Grand River," I demanded, walking out the warehouse with my brothers and Pierre feeling like a weight was lifted off our chests.

Chapter Fifteen

EARLY CHRISTMAS MORNING: PIERRE

Snow was sleep when I came into the house, so I took it upon myself to do something special for my baby. I got the house decorated and put up a real Christmas tree. She hated Christmas, but she didn't have a reason to hate it anymore and I was going to make sure shawty felt the love she deserved. I was going to protect and honor her with my life.

Aaron slid home after we were finished handling Luke's bitch ass and got the presents he said he had for Snow, and brought them to my house. When he came, he and his brothers brought all types of presents.

"Alright bro, I have to get to the crib. It's Christmas, and wifey blowing a nigga line down." He got up and walked to the door, but he ran into Snow. We stood there looking at her because she was supposed to be sleep. Aaron gave her a hug and invited her to Christmas dinner at his house later in the day. She said she would be there, and he and her brothers left.

I closed the door and turned around to Snow staring daggers into me.

"What's going on, Pierre?" she asked as she walked towards the kitchen. She stopped in her tracks when she saw the living room.

The living room looked like a winter wonderland with gifts everywhere and a big ass white tree. The picture of her parents that I had gotten blown up for her was beautiful. Snow stood there frozen, staring, not saying a word. I didn't say anything to her. I just let her take everything in…

Chapter Sixteen

EARLY CHRISTMAS MORNING CONTINUED:
SNOW

Pierre still wasn't at home when I woke up at four in the morning. I was thirsty, so I got out of bed and went downstairs to get a bottle of water out of the refrigerator. When I made it downstairs, I was stopped in my tracks when I saw Aaron standing in my foyer. Seeing him and Pierre kicking it was still weird since they were once enemies. I walked off after Aaron asked if I was coming to Christmas dinner at his house. Of course I told him yes because I didn't want to hear a speech about not being in the holiday spirit.

I walked past the living room and stopped in my tracks. The whole living room was decorated like a wonderland with big, beautiful lights and a Christmas tree with presents everywhere. I started crying when I saw a picture of my parents hanging up. It was beautiful and made me think of my mom and dad and how much I missed them. I walked deeper into the living room and found gifts everywhere. Pierre must have sensed the sadness I was feeling because he didn't say a word. It had to have been at least four o'clock in the morning, but I had so many questions.

"Why are y'all doing this for me?" I asked as I sat down by the fireplace.

"Snow, you deserve to be happy, baby girl, and I need for you to let me do that for you. I want you to start seeing Christmas for what it's really for and that's family, joy, and excitement. You can't go on like this for the rest of your life, Snow. Give it to God. You won't have to worry about anyone hurting you. Luke is dead and that's all you need to know. I know your parents would want you to move on and be happy with your life." Pierre kissed me on the lips, leaving me there to think about what he said... When I turned around, he was gone. I looked out my door and my driveway and only saw my car. I figured he went home and would be back later so I went back to bed and went to sleep.

Chapter Seventeen

IT'S CHRISTMAS: PIERRE

The way I met my long-lost brother was probably the worst way possible to ever be introduced to a sibling. I was lost for words and couldn't nobody be trusted as far as I was concerned. Luke not only killed my woman's parents, but he turned my own brother against me. Killing Luke and Shawn didn't hurt not one bit though. Them grimy ass niggas were never family they were only out for themselves. My beef with Aaron was all based off Luke and his intentions of getting back at Aaron.

Snow Blacc   **Ruby**

After I left Snow in her living room
admiring her Christmas gifts, I went to my house
and showered and changed into my fit for the day.
When I walked to my door, I noticed my mailbox
was full so I checked it. When I looked inside, I had
mail from Friend of the Court. My depression
creeped up because I knew what it was about so I
didn't bother to open it. It was Christmas, I was in
an okay space, and I didn't need shit fucking it up,
at least not today.

After I got everything together, I packed me
a bag for the rest of the week, and tossed my mail in
it. I figured I'd read the letter from FOC with Snow
later. I lounged around my house for a few hours
and made a few Christmas calls to my family. I
didn't even want to call my baby mama to talk to
my son. I knew that bitch probably was on her
bullshit because I had been ignoring her about
Christmas. Last time I gave her money for
Christmas for my son, she blew it on partying. I was

cool on that bitch and that situation, even though I loved my son to pieces.

After chilling for longer than I should have, I headed back to Snow's house before she woke back up. When I walked into Snow's room, she was buried underneath her thick ass comforter.

"Wake up, Snow. Let's go downstairs and open your gifts. I'll cook us a late breakfast to get you energized."

She looked me in the eyes and rolled back over. I snatched the blanket off her and smacked her fat ass, causing her to jump up. She tried to act like she was mad screaming at me, but I didn't care.

"Why you smack my ass like that, boy? You crazy or something?" Snow got out the bed and headed into the bathroom.

While she got herself together, I took my things out my bag and I sat my mail on her vanity set. I went into her kitchen and started cooking bacon, grits, and scrambled eggs with toast. It was finished at the perfect time. Snow entered the kitchen looking beautiful in her silk, purple pajamas. She had a piece of paper in her hand with a frown on her face.

"What's wrong, Snow?" I asked while sitting her plate on the dining room table.

"What's this?" She sat the paper on the table and slid it to me.

"It's papers from Friend of the Court. I already know my payments went up so I don't need to read it."

Snow opened the letter and then jumped up from the table in excitement.

"Oh my god, Pierre, custody was rewarded to you. They found your baby mother unfit to care for your son."

I took the papers out her hand and read what the paper said out loud. I thought I was going bat shit crazy. After all the fighting and court costs, I had finally won.

"I told you to keep the faith, baby." Snow kissed me.

Snow then walked into her living room and started opening her gifts willingly. I stood there watching her face glow as she opened every last one.

"Snow, you were right, and I thank you for helping me. But the same faith you had for me and my case, you need that same faith with believing in Christmas again."

"I think I do now after what you said to me this morning." She smiled. "I feel at ease with Christmas."

I smiled back. "I wanted to go to the movies or something, but let's just chill together before we go to Aaron's dinner. I know since a nigga going to be a full-time dad now, I won't have time to lay up all day with your sexy ass."

"You're going to be a good full-time dad. I think we should go get him today too, he's yours now."

"Yeah, let's do that. I do miss my son and it's Christmas." I was geeked to go get my son for Christmas.

I cleaned up the wrapping paper while Snow was in the shower. I found a red velvet box in back of the tree it had my name on it. I opened it and it was a gold chain. When did Snow have the time to buy me a gift? Especially since she was cool on Christmas for the longest time. I went up to her bedroom and walked in on her slipping on her panties.

"I found your gift for me under the tree. This chain is nice, thank you."

"You're welcome, baby. I didn't want to be a scrooge even before I made a decision on giving Christmas a chance again, so I got you something I knew you would cherish since I know you love gold."

I hugged her tight and kissed her on the lips. Our pecking turned into tongue kissing and everything after that was pure bliss. She felt like putty in my hands every time she got close to me. I couldn't resist her sexy ass every time I saw her naked. I sat her ass up on the dresser. I pulled my dick out and he was already on brick. I loved the look on her face every time I pulled him out. I put her legs on my shoulders and went to work. She was moaning and scratching the fuck out of my back so I bit into her neck and started giving her passion marks. Luckily, she was chocolate so the marks wouldn't be noticeable.

"Yes, Pierre, go deeper. I love it," she begged, and I lost it.

I picked her ass up and fucked her in the air. I walked us over to the bed and laid her down. She got on top and rode my dick like she was a pro. I was getting ready to nut when she came. I put her on all fours and fucked her crazy. I smacked her on the ass, telling her to keep up. I tried to pull out but I couldn't. I released inside of her. She jumped up and frowned at me.

"Damn, Pierre, you know I'm not on birth control. Why would you nut in me?" She smacked her lips.

"Because, I'm trying to put a baby in you." I smiled, making her madder. I knew she didn't want a baby yet, but I did and I wasn't giving up.

"I'm going to take another shower, Pierre. Don't do that anymore."

She turned on the shower and stepped inside. I was ready for a round two, but I knew she didn't have it in her. I joined her, and we washed our bodies. Snow oiled her body down and put on a nude thong and bra. She was so fucking sexy. If she wasn't pregnant now, she was going to be.

Snow walked out of her closet looking like a model in a brown sweater dress with matching thigh high boots. I helped her put on her necklace and matching bracelet. Once we were officially dressed, we headed out the door heading to go get my son and then head to Aaron's.

I pulled up to my baby mother's raggedy ass apartment and felt that feeling in the pit of my stomach like I always did when I came around this bitch. Mayra was a drug addict and she was annoying. I had known her since we were eighteen and she still thought she was eighteen. I got her pregnant because I thought that would change her. I loved her with everything in me because I was a lover. But she betrayed me by sleeping with one of my ex-right-hand men and she stole anything I sat down. I couldn't take it anymore, so I left her. But when I left her, I had to leave my son behind. It's been fighting and a living hell ever since.

I killed the ignition on my brand-new whip and sighed. I still had my hands on the steering wheel. Snow grabbed my hand and held it tight.

"You want me to come in with you?" she asked.

"Nah, I can handle this on my own. This bitch is crazy, and I don't want to put you in harm's way," I admitted.

"Trust me, I may be some schoolgirl lawyer, but I got seven brothers. I can throw them hands."

I chuckled. "I bet you can, but you looking too sexy in my passenger to be fighting."

She laughed. "Well, take this so she can see you were granted full custody. You don't have to wait to see the judge Tuesday for it to be confirmed." She handed me my award letter.

"Alight, I'll be back. Anybody try to fuck with you, my gun is under my seat." I stepped out the car and headed inside the building.

When I walked through her nasty ass building it reeked of trash and old beer cans. I was so disgusted and I had lived in the hood all my life. But Mayra lived in pure filth. This was one of the many reasons my son needed to be with me.

I walked up to her door and it was wide open. When I walked in, her house was trashed. Clothes, liquor bottles, and cocaine residue was on the table.

"Mayra, Jr.!" I shouted through the house and my son darted from the back of the apartment.

"Daddy! I knew you were coming to get me!" my son shouted as he ran into my arms, but I was pissed off when I got a smell of him. It smelled like he hadn't taken a bath in days. I didn't say anything to him though, I just took him into my arms.

"Where your mama at, lil' man? I'm taking you with me." I sat him on the couch in a spot where it looked clean. It looked like Mayra had so much sex on the couch it was crusty with cum stains.

"She's in the back with my other daddy," my son stated, catching me off guard.

"Yo' other daddy?" I frowned. I didn't say anything else to my son. I was on my heels headed to Mayra's room. Before I even approached her room, I heard loud moaning. I pulled my gun from my waist and busted in her room.

"Bitch, you in here fucking and my son all dirty and shit on Christmas Day!" I shouted, letting off a shot through the headboard. I scared the shit out of them both, and they both jumped out the bed.

"Oh my god, Pierre what the fuck are you doing in my house!" Mayra shouted at me, looking like a fucking cracked out hoe. Her weave was matted to her head and her eyes were bloodshot red. She had bruises all over her body and her eye was black.

"Bitch you been letting this nigga beat your ass in front of my son!" I shouted and pulled her to the ground by her nappy weave.

I took my gun and shot at the nigga she was laid up with and sent him running out the apartment naked.

"Bitch, I got awarded full custody of my son, so I'm taking him today!"

"You can't take my son!" she shouted, standing up from the floor. I handed her my paper I got from FOC and that's when all hell broke loose. She started punching and kicking me while she screamed out I wasn't taking my son. One of her punches landed on my jaw and I lost it. I pinned her to her dresser by her throat and everything went flying off of it. "Bitch you been neglecting my son since he's been born. You don't want him so I'm taking him and giving him a good life with my soon-to-be wife!"

"Nigga fuck you and what bitch you fucking! I've been taking care my son alone while you run the streets selling the shit that fucked me up. Get out my house and leave my son here!"

Mayra had to be crazy thinking I was leaving without my Jr. I rushed out her room and headed to the living room. I scooped my son from the couch and headed for the door. When I made it half way to my car, I heard Mayra screaming behind me.

"Fuck you, Pierre, you think you the man, but you ain't nothing but a drug dealing murderer. Do your soon-to-be wife know that!" she continued to shout, but I didn't say anything. I walked to my driver side and opened the back door to put my son in.

"Don't listen to your mama, lil' man. You don't have to worry anymore. You're coming with me for good."

That's when I heard her yelling at Snow through the window.

"You think you the shit, bitch, because you fucking this nigga? You think he got money and it's legit huh? Trust me, hoe, you ain't the only one, while you sitting there thinking your black ass is pretty. I know that dick good, bitch, it used to belong to me, hoe. All down my throat, you ugly ass bitch! Get out the car, lil' girl. I'll fuck you up!"

I heard the door from my passenger fly open and looked up. Snow opened the door, knocking Mayra on her ass. Snow bent down before Mayra could get up and started punching her in the face.

"Bitch, well he's my fucking nigga now and if I catch you trying to fuck over my man and his son, I'll fuck you up again!" Snow shouted.

I ran over to her side of the car and snatched Snow off Mayra. I tossed her in the passenger as Mayra continued to shout. I got in the driver side and drove off.

"Yo, Snow, I thought I told you to stay in the car," I said, almost out of breath as I did 80 down the street. I saw a cop, so I slowed down.

"You thought I was going to sit there and let that bitch yell at me, Pierre? You must not really know me like you say," Snow said in a tone I had never heard before.

I sat there quiet, thinking about how Snow really had my back.

"You held your shit babe and thanks for taking up for a nigga but you don't need to be fighting, especially since you are back in the Christmas spirit again."

She sighed. "You're right, but nothing will ever kill my spirit again. Let's just go to my brother's house and make sure they don't find out about this."

I nodded. "You got it, but first I gotta go clean my son up and give him his gifts."

We slid back to my crib and Snow helped me get my son ready. Well actually, she did everything while I made a few calls about this bitch Mayra to my family. Snow bathed him, dressed him in a new fit I had for him, and cooked him a quick breakfast. After that, we stood in my living room watching my son open his gifts. I looked over at Snow as she looked at my son open his gift. I knew Snow would make a good mother one day, just on the strength of how much of a good person she was. I couldn't wait to start a family with her with my son because I knew our kids would be well taken care of when I'm not around…

Chapter Eighteen
CHRISTMAS DINNER: AARON

After killing Luke and Shawn, I felt like a weight was lifted off my chest. I finally had my family back, and on top of it all, I gained a brother-in-law. I planned a Christmas dinner at my house and I was glad Snow agreed to come, especially after what happened at her surprise party. I knew it threw her off when she saw me at her house helping Pierre out.

After I left Snow's house, I made it home in record time and Desari was up cooking at five in the

morning. The house smelled lovey, and it made me
think back when my mother and Snow used to cook
Christmas dinner. My wife was big on Christmas,
so I jumped in the shower, changed my clothes, and
helped her.

"Hey, baby." I kissed her on the cheek and
sat down to watch her make pies.

"Good morning, Aaron." She leaned over to
kiss me. "I know you just got in and I'm not mad at
you. You had to do what was needed and I'm proud
of you. I just hope Snow can find her way now and
stop grieving. It's time for her to heal."

"I just left her house, and I'm sure Pierre is
going to talk to her. She said she would be here
tonight, so that's a start."

My wife nodded. "Well now that you are
here, I'm going to lay down. I been up cooking all
night and I feel sick. Please don't let my pies burn,
Aaron."

I let my wife sleep while I finished cooking dinner. I went to wake my wife up so she could get ready for our guests.

"Wake up, bae, it's almost 7 pm." I shook her lightly.

After sitting up for another fifteen minutes, Desari finally got up and got dressed. She then came out the bathroom and had a whole meltdown that she slept the whole day away and hadn't talked to any of her family members.

"Calm down, baby. I finished everything so you could get some sleep. You been working hard all day." I kissed her and walked out of the bathroom. I headed downstairs to get the good china out the cabinets. Desari came downstairs dressed in a red, silk dress pants outfit. The doorbell started ringing and I knew it was my siblings so I got happy as hell. Once everyone showed up dinner was served...

Snow Blacc   Ruby

LATER THAT EVENING

Everyone showed up to the house ready to eat and drink. For the first time in eight years we all were back under one roof and that's all I wanted for Christmas. I looked at the ceiling thanking God and my parents that my siblings and I reunited. Paul and Lysa were all hugged up and Snow and Pierre looked happy with his son. It was a sight to remember.

We ate dinner and reminisced on our Christmas as kids. Everybody at the dinner had a gift to open including Pierre. I saw Snow open her gift and cry. She got up from the table excusing herself. Desari and Lysa went to check on her.

While the ladies were gone, us men chatted real quick, killing time. We all pitched in and got her a real gold locket with the words "Forever blessed" with a picture in it we took in 2003 as a whole family.

"Thank you, brothers, I really appreciate my gift," Snow said when she came back in the room.

After sitting and drinking at the dinner table, I got up from the table and made an announcement. Desari smacked her lips and I bent down to kiss her. She thought I was going to probably say some long speech, but I wasn't.

"This New Year's Eve I will be hosting a masquerade ball and everybody that's in this room going," I told everybody sipping my champagne, sitting back down.

Chapter Nineteen
NEW YEAR'S EVE: SNOW

It was New Year's Eve, and I had my head in the toilet bowl. The bug was going around, and it finally caught up with me. I tried my hardest to avoid it after Lysa got sick at work. Pierre walked into the bathroom and handed me a can of ginger ale but I was too scared to drink it. He rubbed my back as I threw up the lining of my stomach. I couldn't take it anymore; I needed to go to the medical center. I looked at Pierre crying, trying to talk in between throwing up.

"Can you please take me to the hospital or something? I can't take this feeling any longer," I babbled in between throwing up. After getting dressed Pierre picked his car keys of the nightstand by the bed helping me to the car. He looked worried.

"Snow, are you sure you're not pregnant?" Pierre joked while eying me. He helped me into the car. He was joking but I didn't see anything funny about it.

The drive to the medical center was quick and I was glad because I started throwing up again. I was beyond feeling weak. I couldn't walk into the center; he had to grab a wheelchair for me. After checking in it felt like we sat in the waiting room for hours. I was feeling like shit by the minute. I was getting ready to go home when I heard my name getting called.

"Snow Blacc," a white, old nurse called me back asking a thousand and one questions. She took my vitals and temperature and I had a high fever.

"What brings you in, Ms. Blacc?" she asked with concerned eyes.

"Christmas night I started to feel sick. I barely ate anything because it made me queasy. I think I have the flu. My sister-in-law had a 24-hour bug so I think that's where I got it from," I said looking at Pierre sitting there worried.

When she asked was it possible I could be pregnant, I looked at her as if she was crazy. Every time around this year I made myself sick working so much and stressing. I froze at the thought, trying to remember my last period but I honestly didn't know. I knew I wasn't pregnant so that question was out the window. I looked at her before answering her.

"I'm not pregnant, I would know that, it's my body," I whispered.

"Well I just need for you to pee in this cup so we can make sure," she said while handing me a bag with a cup and three wipes in it.

I glared at Pierre while getting off the bed heading into the bathroom to pee. I swore to God I wasn't pregnant.

When I returned to the room, the nurse gave me nausea medicine. It helped with the sick feeling but I still felt queasy a little bit. We waited for what seemed like hours before the doctor and nurse came back into my room. When they told me I was pregnant, all I could do was cry. I wasn't ready for kids yet.

Pierre looked nervous so I stayed quiet during the ultrasound. I was indeed seven weeks pregnant. Seeing that little bean on the screen made my heart melt. I had a human growing inside of me.

After being discharged with instructions, we went home. I noticed Pierre had been quiet since he found out I was pregnant. But I didn't say anything either. I was going to let him address the situation when he was ready.

Chapter Twenty
BEFORE THE BALL
DROPS: PIERRE

Finding out Snow was pregnant wasn't a shock to me. The second time me and shawty fucked I didn't strap up so I knew the baby was mine. I never doubted it one time. I started to figure she was pregnant at her party. She kept complaining about feeling queasy but I brushed it off. I can't lie; a nigga was happy. I got the court judgement papers in the mail about my case. I had won full custody of my son and I was more than happy. Everything I ever wanted for Christmas I got all in one week. I gained a new friendship with an old enemy and I got the girl of my dreams with a baby on the way. I was sitting on a high horse.

I looked at myself in the mirror dressed in all black. I haven't been this happy in a minute and Snow was the reason. I went to check on her to make sure she was comfortable in bed before I left out for the night to celebrate. When I walked in, she was dressed in a beautiful purple gown which took me by surprise because she was sick as hell. Looking at her, you couldn't tell if she was sick or not. I stared at her until she spoke.

"Why are you looking at me like that, Pierre?" she asked, putting on a silver necklace to match her earrings.

"Damn, can a nigga look at your sexy ass before you start going off? I thought you weren't going, why are you out of bed, Snow?" I sat on the bed.

Snow Blacc   **Ruby**

"For the last eight years it's been hell on earth trying to deal with the fact that I'll never see my parents again and I hated myself for years because I felt like I could have done something, and they'd still be here. You killing Luke for me opened my eyes and I need to properly grieve and move on with my life and I'm trying to do just that. I'm getting ready to have my own family. I don't want to carry this burden any longer. So I'm going out to be with my family, sick or not. I'll be okay with all of my family around."

Snow had officially broken down and let it all out. She stood there balling her eyes out and I let her. She needed to let all that hurt go.

"Even though I'm sick, I won't let my man bring in New Year's without me and our little peanut." She pointed to her stomach. It made a nigga feel warm inside.

We made our way to the New Year's masquerade ball after I dropped my son to my

mother. Walking in there with Snow on my arm
made me feel like a king. All eyes were on us and I
knew she felt that shit too.

We finally met up with her brothers and the
ladies. The Blacc family was finally reunited and
Snow had finally found her hood prince charming. I
had to make an announcement before the ball
dropped. I pulled Aaron and his brothers to the side,
letting them know what was up and to ask for their
blessing to marry Snow.

"Snow, can you please come to the stage?"
my voice boomed through the speakers getting
everyone's attention. I saw her being escorted
through the crowed by her seven brothers. My heart
felt like it was about to jump out my chest. I had a
whole speech prepared for her. It was fifteen
minutes before the ball dropped.

"Snow, the first time I ran into you,
knocking you down, I knew you would be the one.
You were spicy and a fresh breath of air a nigga

needed. I know we haven't been together that long but you make me happy and I know you been through some shit and I'm here to let you know you don't have to worry about a thing but living your life stress free. I want to wake up to your beautiful smile every morning. I want to be your king and I plan to make you my queen since I already made you a mother. I want all of my kids to grow up under one roof. And with that being said, Snow Blacc, will you marry me?" I blurted out loud and proud.

All the females gasped with tears in their eyes.

"Yes," Snow beamed with excitement.

"We have another announcement," Snow yelled out. Everybody's attention was focused on us anyway, so I let Snow fill them in.

"As some of you heard in Pierre's speech, he said something about kids. Well I want everyone to know we are expecting a child in the next seven months."

Everyone in the room cheered for us. Desari and Lysa were shocked that Snow was pregnant. Aaron waved for me and Snow so we made our way towards him. Aaron and his brothers stood there glaring at me and Snow.

"We just wanted to congratulate y'all on the engagement and the new bundle of joy you are now carrying, Snow. Mom and Dad would be proud of you if they were here, baby girl. If anybody deserves to be happy, it's you." Aaron's voice started to crack. I knew her seven brothers meant every word they said.

After all seven of them gave Snow a hug it was time to count down for a new year. When the count started, I noticed Snow was crying again so I had to ask her was she okay.

"I'm okay, Pierre. I'm happy. I haven't been
this happy in years and now I can finally be free and
live. Thank you for making me believe again."
Snow kissed me soon as the ball dropped. I finally
had my happy ending.

The End...

**MERRY CHRISTMAS
& HAPPY NEW YEAR**

Coming soon from Ruby

CPSIA information can be obtained
at www.ICGtesting.com
Printed in the USA
LVHW091314221119
638185LV00001B/71/P

9 781792 166464